FOREVER YOURS, KITTEN

EMILIA ROSE

Cover by: The Book Brander

Editing by: Jovana Shirley, Unforeseen Editing, www.unforeseenediting.com

Proofreading by: Zainab M., Heart Full of Reads Editing Services

Emilia Rose

emiliarosewriting@gmail.com

To everyone who's supported me over the years.

TRIGGER WARNING

This book contains dark themes, such as self-harming, memories of sexual assault, violence, death, and loss. If these are trigger topics for you, I suggest not reading further.

CHAPTER 1

AURORA

"*D*o you think you'd ever be able to tame the hounds?" a beautiful woman from my left said to me. Sunlight glinted in her dark eyes, and strands of her indigo hair blew gently into her sallow, cadaverous face.

I lay back in a field filled with moonflowers and breathed in the fresh scent of dew on the leaves and grass, my mind buzzing with hundreds upon hundreds of thoughts about those charming wild animals.

Taming the hounds? There was no such thing. Why would someone ever think that I could tame them as I was? Those beasts might love spending time with me, but they were wild animals and shouldn't be tamed for war or violence. They should do as they pleased.

But an unspoken war had been brewing, and I'd wanted to save them from it for so long now. I glanced over at the woman with indigo hair and smiled. She was the only person who knew how much those creatures loved me and my undying love for them.

"Maybe one day," I whispered.

Maybe if I tried hard enough or loved hard enough, I might be able to tame those monsters. But I would never truly know because I didn't belong in the depths of the underworld, where they lived during the darkest of nights. I belonged under the sun and moon, with my family in these woods.

Sunlight flooded the field, flickering through the surrounding trees in the Sanguine Wilds and glistening against a couple of rogue wolves' fur in the forest. My breath caught in my throat as they ambled through the woods toward me, their usual deadly and vicious expressions softening when their gazes landed on me.

I sat up and watched the beasts with a flutter in my heart.

The woman sat up beside me and smiled. "One day? All the wolves in the Sanguine Wilds love you. Why don't you think they'd love you in the underworld too? They might be vicious creatures, but all they need is to be tamed. And the ones who pay you a visit in this world love you so much more than these rogues do."

Something in her voice didn't sit right with me, but I trusted her—maybe a bit too much. "I'd rather not go to the underworld. My home is here. My life is here. My brother and sister are here, and so are these wolves."

The rogues hurried a bit faster toward me; the wind blowing through their thick fur. When they reached the edge of the forest, right before the moonflower field, they sprinted and leaped in my direction. Instead of shielding my face and rolling out of the way from their attack, I let them jump onto me and lick my face with their coarse tongues.

One put his head in my lap, piercing golden eyes staring up at me. I rested my palm against his ratty fur and smoothed it out, loathing how knotty he had made it since the last time I had seen him. Rogues deserved more than this, so much more.

"The wolves are your sister's creation," the woman said. "They worship her, not you. You should have a species of your own to tame and make them fight for you. You should have a species to call your

own. *Your bond with beasts and monsters is so great that sometimes, I mistake you for a goddess from the underworld."*

"Not all wolves like me, Nyx," I said, smiling down at the beast. "Just the broken ones."

I didn't have any problem with my sister having the wolves as hers. I just gave the rogues a little extra love because that was what they deserved. They hadn't asked for a lonely life, but that was what they had been given by their peers, and I understood how hard it was to be alone.

"Fine." Nyx pursed her lips and stared down at the moonflowers ... angrily.

I didn't know what I'd said to make her so furious. She knew that I would never leave this world to live with those awful gods in the underworld.

"So, how's Ares?"

"Ares?" I asked, brow furrowed.

Something about this suddenly didn't seem right, and I realized I didn't really know who this woman was or why she was asking about Ares. He was the one person who could bring me back to reality, the one person who should never be asked about by a random woman with indigo hair.

"Don't play dumb. Ares, as in your secret lover?"

My heart raced, and I glanced around the field, trying to find any trace of Ares's scent or to find him watching me the way he always did to make sure I was okay, but he was nowhere to be seen. I was alone out here with someone I suddenly didn't recognize, someone those gods had warned me about.

"Why're you freaking out?" Nyx asked, grasping my hand. Her touch was so cold and chilling that I recoiled. She moved closer, the sun dancing in her eyes like a single spark of hope. But her irises were so dark they nearly consumed all light. "Are you okay?"

The wolves around me cuddled closer, and I found myself taking a huge breath of fresh morning air. I relaxed further against the wolves, memories that I knew I had never experienced with Ares rushing through my mind. This wasn't my life; I was sure that this wasn't real.

It could be a figment of my imagination or a memory that I'd sort of ... unlocked from whoever the hell had had this stone inside of them before me. That was the only way that this could be, right? Unless ... this was all a dream.

A flaming chariot led by horses with wings on fire flew through the air. A man leaning over the edge smiled down at me and waved.

"Dawn." He nodded to me and then let his gaze linger a bit too long on the beautiful woman beside me. "Nyx."

"Morning, Helios," Nyx said, a slight smile curling on her face.

Helios landed his golden chariot in the clearing on the edge of the field and hopped out of it, running his fingers across the horses' silky coat without burning himself with their raging fire. "You stayed?" Helios said to Nyx, one brow raised slightly. "You said you were leaving."

"I wanted to talk to my best friend," Nyx said, gaze playfully narrowing.

Best friend? Nyx is my best friend?

"You guys saw each other last night?" I asked, staring between her and him.

They both looked surprised, as if I should've already known that they were together. It was obvious in the way that they interacted, their light and darkness clashing and bouncing off each other.

Helios narrowed his gaze at me, eyes intense, as if he was scolding me. "No," he said, but his eyes said otherwise. He walked closer to me, making the rogue in my lap stand over me in a protective manner, and then he lowered his voice. "You know not to say it out loud."

It was a secret.

What other secrets did I have? What secrets was I supposed to keep? Did gods keep secrets? Was I talking to gods themselves? Who even was I, and what was I doing here? Where was my Ares? Why wasn't he here, watching me closely, like he always did?

I needed him right now.

4

"Ares?" I asked, unable to hold myself back from saying his name. "Where's Ares?"

I had so many damn questions that neither of these people could answer. Had I lived for thousands of years? And who the hell was Nyx? I had never seen her before, but I felt such a connection with her.

Helios's horses neighed loudly, as if they were ready to leave.

Helios hopped back into his chariot and grabbed the reins. "I'll see you tomorrow. I have to go fly across the sky."

The chariot lifted into the air, the wind from the horses' wings flapping and making the rogues' fur sway in the breeze.

Nyx stood. "I have to go too, back to the underworld. If I'm gone for too long, my brother, Erebus, will come looking for me," she said. "Then, he'll start asking questions." She looked up at the sun and squinted. "And I can't have him asking questions about my whereabouts or about your brother."

When they both ran off, I lay back in the meadow again, my gaze shifting between Helios in his flaming chariot and the moon fading in the sunlight. More rogues walked out from the forest, lying around me— one with his snout in the crook of my arm, another with his paw on my thigh. I stroked the rogues' fur, my fingers curling into it.

"One day, I will tame the hounds," I found myself saying. "One day, I'll save them."

I WOKE up in my mother's old king-size bed, with my chest heaving up and down, and a thick layer of sweat rolling down my back. My stomach twisted into knots, and I felt both disturbed and startled at the mere memory.

Because that dream had felt real.

It wasn't something my mind could have fabricated unless my pregnant ass had some weird fantasies or something. Though I was almost sure that this hadn't been just a dream, and it was beyond odd, looking into intimate memories that weren't my own, but feeling as if they were.

Something about them made me smile yet recoil in horror.

Everything had seemed a bit too fine in that world—wherever or *whenever* it was. Nyx, the goddess who wanted to kill me now, was my best friend. She and Helios were hooking up. Helios was somehow my … brother. And Nyx had desperately wanted me to live in the underworld with her for some reason.

Orange sunlight flooded in through the thin, sheer curtains. Ruffles shifted on my stomach, curling around my growing baby bump and resting her head right over my navel, like she was listening to the baby inside.

"*Meow,*" she purred, voice chirpy.

"Can you hear my baby?" I whispered down at her, careful not to wake a sleeping Ares.

"*Meow.*"

"I know." I stroked Ruffles's gray fur like I had stroked those rogues in my dream, my fingers remembering how knotty and unkempt their fur had been in my palms and how calm their mere presence had made me. "She's growing quickly."

"*Meow.*"

I ran my other hand over my bump. While humans tended to have their babies within a nine-month period, werewolves had their babies in three months, which meant that our baby would be here sooner rather than later, and we were not prepared in the slightest.

My bump was still small enough that it could be hidden with the right kind of dress. It'd probably stay that way until about a week before the baby was supposed to be born—at least, that was how Mom had told me her pregnancy was with Jeremy.

Wanting to forget about her and my dream, I slipped out of bed. "Come on, Ruffles. Let's do our morning routine before Ares wakes up. You still remember it from when we used to live here, right?"

Ruffles licked my nose with her rough tongue and hopped off the bed, her pregnant belly nearly brushing against the ground as she headed toward the door for our morning stroll to the porch to watch nature at its finest. We tiptoed past my old room, where Marcel and Charolette were now staying, and walked down the creaky stairs to the porch.

When I opened the front door, we both squinted our eyes at the blazing sun. I glanced up at the sky, wondering if Helios—that man from my dreams and the God from the hound fight a couple weeks ago—really was driving his golden chariot across the sky. But Helios was in the underworld, trapped and fighting for our lives.

Shaking the thought away, I followed Ruffles to our rocking chairs on the porch. Instead of jumping on hers, she sprawled out in the sun, her little mouth pulled into a joyous smile. She rolled onto her back to sunbathe and chirped along with the birds.

My lips curled into a small smile, and I glanced around the front yard, remembering the way that Jeremy used to chase me around, how we would play with all the pack pups all day long. One time, we had even come home with dirt and sticks in our hair before dinner.

That day was the first time I'd heard Mom scold Jeremy, and I'd never forget it because Jeremy was always the prized and praised child. Sometimes, Mom treated me so badly that I couldn't even fathom I was her child.

She'd never treated Jeremy as poorly as she treated me.

As I stared out into the desolate and quiet forest, I wondered if Mom would've treated me any differently if I'd had the power I did now. Would she have appreciated that I could shift? Would she have loved that I could heal not only myself but also other people? Or would she have used me for her own selfish desires?

I balled my hands into fists, feeling both immense sorrow and pain firing through me. I would never fucking know the answers to those questions because like the majority of my old packmates, she was dead now.

She'd never come back.

And if Fenris somehow brought her back from the dead, I would relish in killing her hound body. Dad would hate me for it, but he wasn't here either. They had both left me to die because I was nothing to them.

Suddenly, to my left, a figure moved in the forest. Ruffles and I both sat up taller to get a better look, my heart racing at the thought of hounds. They hadn't shown up in two long weeks, and every day, I feared that they would show up stronger and faster than before.

"Ruffles," I whispered, "if this is a hound, run back into that house and get Ares."

Ruffles stood on all fours, her teeth drawn and a growl rumbling from her throat.

The figure moved between two trees and finally revealed himself to me, standing naked and suspended in time. I froze in the spot, my entire body tensing and an indescribable feeling shooting through my limbs.

No, this can't be. It really can't be him, can it?

"*Kitten,*" a distant voice drifted through the mindlink.

"Mars ..."

CHAPTER 2

ARES

"*A baby, Ares?*" *Aurora asked, staring up at me with eyes a sea of soft pinks, oranges, and yellows—the true colors of the dawn that flooded across the Sanguine Wilds before the sunlight overwhelmed the forest and life awakened—but not the eye color of* my *Aurora. "You want to have a baby?"*

I wrapped my arms around her smaller waist, lifting her into the air and spinning her around, her long brown hair swinging. She tossed her head back and giggled, the sweet sounds getting lost in the wind.

"Yes, I want a child with you," I said against the column of her neck, kissing her. "It's all I've wanted for the past thousand years."

When I finally placed her back down on the ground, she brushed her fingers through my hair and grinned. "Of course I want to have a baby with you," she whispered, her gaze suddenly falling to the trees surrounding us, her forehead creasing. "But Hella ... she's after us."

"She doesn't matter, Kitten," I said. "I'll protect you from her."

Aurora stepped away from me and shook her head. "We can't, Ares."

Rogue wolves approached from all directions in the woods,

surrounding Aurora and eventually sitting at her feet. She crouched down between them, running her slender fingers across their ratty fur and staring up at me.

"We can't let her control our lives forever," I said, feeling the anger pool inside me.

Mars had told me to ask Aurora about having a child without fury and rage building, and I had fucking tried. But that was who I was, and I couldn't act like someone I wasn't. Aurora was with me because I was the god of war and would protect her, no matter what.

She needed to know I would do anything for her.

"I would kill those gods with my own two hands if they came close to you or our baby."

"You can't kill gods," Aurora said, clenching her jaw. "They've tried to kill me so many times, Ares, if you don't remember." Suddenly, Aurora stood back up, her stare hardening into a menacing glare, and then she pulled down the front of her dress, enough for me to see the scars on her chest.

Fifteen.

At least.

In various stages of healing, the pink scars lined her skin across her chest, gathering near her heart. Had Hella and Nyx already tried to kill her multiple times? Why hadn't the scars healed yet? Were they permanently on her skin?

"Do you remember these?" Aurora asked me with tears in her eyes. She brushed her fingers over a huge circular scar in the center of her chest. "This one was with Hella's magic, only a couple moments after you left for war."

She moved to an inch-long scar toward the left that looked like it had been caused by an arrow. "This one was when I traveled with you to help fight in the war against the Trojans. You fought man after man while Hella pierced me with one of the Trojans' arrows."

Then, her fingers grazed against the scar right over her heart. "And this … you must remember this one, Ares."

Swallowing hard, I nodded. "That was the wound I couldn't protect you from."

A tear slid down Aurora's cheek. She crouched back down in the pile of rogues and lay back, her head on one of their bellies and her frown quivering. "I don't blame you for not being able to protect me. Hella was resourceful and used your spear against you, but ... I ..." She paused for a long time. "If we had a baby, we'd need to protect her, too. I might be able to survive a divine attack, but a baby wouldn't."

"I'm sorry," I said, balling my hands into fists.

I wasn't fucking good enough to protect her. I'd fucking let Hella hurt her.

It was my fault. My fucking fault.

I wasn't good enough or fast enough or strong enough.

"I'm so sorry, Aurora."

"Aurora?" she asked, glaring up at me with wide, rageful eyes. "Who's Aurora?"

"You," I whispered.

"I'm not Aurora, Ares. I'm Dawn."

* * *

"MARS." Aurora sat in a field of moonflowers with her hand resting on her swollen belly and glanced at me with those colorful eyes shifting between pink, orange, and yellow. "Come here. Feel our daughter kick."

Covered in the taste of war, I walked out from the woods and through the field. The flowers twinkled against my shins, creating a wave of light in the darkest of the night. A couple of rogue wolves sat by Aurora's side, resting their snouts against her thighs. When I approached, they parted to make a path for me.

I knelt by her side and ran my fingers across her stomach. Aurora placed her hand over mine and guided it toward the top of her belly; her flushed cheeks rounded. Our baby kicked my hand with her small feet, and I held back my tears.

This was actually happening.

We were really having a baby after thousands of years.

"Did you feel that?" Aurora asked.

"Our girl," I whispered.

"You know, we need to pick out a name," she said, puckering her lips and wanting a kiss.

After kissing her, I sat by her side and stared up at the stars decorating the night. "I've been thinking about a few. What about—"

Before I could get a word out, a branch snapped in the woods about a mile away. The rogues lifted their heads and stared in the southeast direction, baring their saliva-covered canines. I stood in front of Aurora with my head held high.

I would do anything to protect Aurora and my baby.

Anything.

Shooting through the air, an arrow whizzed right by me, grazing me against the cheek and drawing blood. I growled at the forest, feeling the power swell through my body, and beckoned my inner beast.

Anything for Aurora.

Another arrow whizzed by, hitting me in the right bicep, and then another pierced through my right thigh.

I narrowed my eyes, vision enhancing, and stared at Hella from across the forest, shooting arrows at us with that vile expression written all over her old, ugly face. Balling my hands into fists, I watched the last of her arrows shoot through the air, aimed at nothing other than Aurora's swollen belly.

Squeezing her eyes closed, Aurora screamed and held her arms over her stomach. I reached out at just the last moment and grabbed the arrow right in the air, millimeters before it made contact with her.

Heart racing, I snapped the arrow into two pieces, grabbed my spear near the edge of the woods, aimed it at Hella, and launched it faster than I had ever thrown a spear. "Nobody hurts my family."

* * *

Two big pink, orange, and yellow eyes stared up at me, the colors dancing in the early morning sunlight. In the field of moonflowers, I lay on my back and held my daughter in the air above me, listening to a giggle escape her toothless mouth. Our baby gently grasped my thumb in her tiny palm and squeezed harder than any baby I had held.

She would be stronger than both Aurora and me one day. I didn't doubt it.

While she babbled to me, a wad of spit dripped out of her mouth and landed with a splat on my cheek. A chuckle rolled through my chest, and she giggled, too, her eyes scrunching up the way Aurora's did, and her little body rumbling.

Rogue wolves walked out through the forest and into the field at the sound of her voice. One sat down beside us and stared up at me through wide black eyes, as if to ask if he could see her. I sat up and placed our baby on the ground beside him.

She crawled over to him and collapsed against his fur, her head on his abdomen and her tiny fingers reaching out to touch his snout. He licked her fingers, and she let out another heartwarming giggle.

I stared down at our girl, a warmth spreading throughout my chest.

Thank the gods that Mars had convinced Aurora to have a child.

This was the best damn thing to happen to me.

Drawing her finger across his canine tooth, she grasped it in her hand and widened her colorful eyes, fascinated with him, just like her mother was. More rogues approached from the woods from the south, followed by Aurora.

"Someone's having fun," she said, grinning at us with her long brown hair blowing in her face. She walked over and picked up our daughter, rocking her in her arms.

Our baby wrapped her arms around Aurora's shoulders and rested her head right over Aurora's heart.

I smiled at my two girls, nothing but pride and happiness rushing through me.

These girls were my—

Suddenly, a spear—one of my old spears—flew through the air, spiraling toward Aurora. I shot up from the moonflower field and lunged at Aurora to push her out of the way, but the pike thrust through her heart and straight through our baby.

Aurora collapsed almost immediately, her eyes wide and blood pouring out of her wound. I fell to my knees and shook my head from side to side.

"No! No. No. No. No. No. No. No!" I shouted.

"The baby," Aurora said, voice hoarse. "Help the baby."

But our once-smiling baby girl was now ... nothing but a corpse.

"No!" I screamed, tears flowing down my cheeks. "No!"

Aurora stared up at me through watery eyes, not moving any part of her body, not even her head enough to see our child lying dead in her arms. "How is she?" Aurora asked. "I can't move. Is she okay?"

Mars had easily protected Aurora and our child many times. Hella had attacked me once with my own spear, and I couldn't fucking save my own family. I was a failure, a fucking failure as a father and as a mate.

Aurora would never forgive me for this.

I would fail to be a good father in every lifetime.

"Ares," Aurora said, "answer me."

After brushing some hair off her sweaty forehead, I sobbed. "She's dead, Aurora. Dead."

CHAPTER 3

AURORA

*M*ars hurried back through the forest, away from me and toward the lake, sneaking through the hidden cave that only I knew about, climbing around a small cliff, and moving his large frame between close rocks to come to a clearing at the lake.

I squeezed my pregnant body between the rocks, desperate to follow and see him again.

But the closer we approached the lake, the quicker his pace became. I pumped my legs faster to keep up and shielded my face with my hand, the reflection of the sparkling sun against the blue lake too bright.

Tree bark, leaves, and twigs scraped against my legs, but I didn't care. And neither did Ruffles because she was right by my side, following me every single step of the way to see Mars again.

When I emerged through the shaggy, verdant trees, Mars stood at the base of the lake with his beautiful, crooked smile that always made my heart warm.

"No matter where I am, I'll forever be with you."

"Mars," I whispered, taking another step toward him.

"Forever yours, Kitten," he said, brushing his fingers against my baby bump.

And while I'd expected his touch to be warm, I couldn't feel anything. I reached out for him, aching to hug him again, but my arms swiped right through his ghostly body. Little by little, Mars disappeared right in front of me, his body turning to dust, small particles drifting out over the water, so small that I couldn't even grasp them in my hands.

A hopeless cry escaped through my parted lips as I stared out into the nothingness in front of me, my stomach in knots and tears pouring down my cheeks. This was all just ... a cruel joke my mind had played on me.

I had been chasing a ghost. Mars was gone.

"*Meow*," Ruffles said beside me, rubbing against my legs.

Defeat hollowed out my insides and crushed me to my very core.

Needing someone, I picked her up, hugged her close to my chest, and walked away from the place I had met Mars. Ruffles rested her head on my shoulder and watched the lake disappear from her view.

Once I finally made it back to the pack house, I placed Ruffles down and wiped my tears, refusing to let Ares see how broken not having Mars around had made me. Ares had spent all his life with Mars. I didn't have a fraction of the pain he must be carrying.

Stepping into the house with a fake smile on my face, I found Marcel and Charolette in the kitchen, making breakfast. Marcel stood behind Charolette, his arms around her waist, pulling her closer as she giggled and flipped a couple fluffy pancakes with a spatula.

With his silver hair falling into his face, he buried his head into the crook of her neck and mumbled something into her ear.

I smiled at them, my stomach doing flips at the thought of them finally being happy together, and decided not to interrupt their moment.

"Aurora, no," Ares said from our bedroom.

I hurried toward the bedroom to check on Ares. Ever since Mars had died, nightmares had been plaguing every bit of his sleep. And I was terrified that if he didn't talk to someone soon, they would seize control of him and force him to slip into the darkness again.

Ares lay in our bed, squeezing his eyes closed and twisting his head from side to side. "No," he mumbled in his sleep. A bead of sweat rolled down his neck and onto his white Sanguine Wilds T-shirt "Stop. No."

I furrowed my brows slightly and gently sat beside him, brushing some dark brown hair off his forehead. "Ares, wake up," I whispered, my heart aching.

Ruffles jumped onto my side of the bed and sashayed over to his face, licking his sweat off him.

But he still didn't calm down, so I nudged him again. "Ares, wake up."

"Goddess, stop," he whispered. "Please, stop. I don't want to see it again. I can't see this again." More sweat formed at the nape of his neck, his entire body violently trembling so hard that the headboard started banging against the wall. "Aurora ... don't touch Aurora."

Deciding that this wasn't working, I straddled his waist and pinned my hands against his shoulders to stop him from freaking out. "Ares, stop," I pleaded, desperate for him to stop it now. This was the third morning that I had to force him awake.

And whenever I woke him and asked about his nightmares, he lied to me. He acted as if his dreams had been filled with moon-flowers, the Moon Goddess, or his good memories about his mother. Nothing out of the ordinary, nothing making him so anxious during the day that he couldn't focus.

He was hiding the truth from me, and it hurt damn bad. But I knew that this was what Ares did. He had tried to hide the truth from Mars to protect him, and now, he was doing it with me too. Only this time, it was taking a toll on him because he lived in this nightmare twenty-four hours a day, seven days a week.

Mars was gone.

"Ares, wake up," I whispered, placing my lips against his and trying hard to pull him awake, to give him some good, so his life wasn't filled with unpleasant thoughts of losing his other half.

I didn't know what was truly going on between Mars and Ares, but I did know that mental illness couldn't be fixed with just a kiss. It wasn't a fairy tale; it was a hound rearing its ugly head, ready to tear someone apart any moment of any day—even in their dreams.

Ares relaxed slightly yet still mumbled the word, "No," over and over again.

I grabbed one of his hands and placed it right over my bump, where our pup grew. Ares stirred slightly, his body relaxing against the mattress.

When the corner of his lip curled into a smile and he slowly blinked his eyes open, I finally took a deep, relaxing breath. It had taken longer to wake him than it usually did.

"Morning, Kitten."

I furrowed my brows. "Are you okay?"

He wrapped his big, strong arms around my waist and pulled me to his chest, grinding his hips against mine until he got hard. "I'm fine."

"You're not fine, Ares," I murmured.

"Well then, make me fine." He sucked my bottom lip between his teeth and grasped a fistful of my hair in his hand, pulling it backward until I was looking down at him. His hard cock glided against my thin shorts. "Come on, Kitten. I can smell your pretty, wet cunt."

He slid his hand down my backside, slapped my ass hard, and

gripped it in his hand. All I could feel was the wetness pooling between my legs and the heat between my thighs.

He rubbed his cock against my pussy and groaned against my lips. "Fuck..."

Rolling us over, he wrapped his arms underneath my thighs and pressed his lips against his mark, sucking on the skin and making me moan. This was his way to keep me quiet, to shut me up so I wouldn't ask about his nightmares.

"Ares, we can't." I gently pushed on his chest. "We have ... have people ..."

"People what, Kitten?" he murmured against me, his breath hot against the column of my throat. He placed sloppy kisses down my body, his hands sliding under my shirt and groping my breasts. "Hmm?"

"Your therapist will be over soon," I whispered.

"She's coming after breakfast." He yanked down my shorts and underwear. "I want to be inside of you now."

He stuck two fingers into my pussy and dipped his head between my legs, spreading my folds, spitting on my clit, and flicking his tongue against it. I squirmed in his hold as he grazed his tongue over and over against my core in small, torturous circles, his fingers pumping in and out of me in a cruel, rhythmic motion.

"Ares! Aurora!" Charolette shouted from the kitchen. "Breakfast is ready!"

"We'll be out in a minute," Ares said back, not caring if she heard or not.

I shifted under him, trying to displace all the pressure inside my core. It was building higher, pushing me closer and closer to the edge of coming undone underneath him.

And while I wanted Ares to open up to me about what he'd been struggling with, this was sorta my way of dealing with everything going on around us too. I wanted to escape in the feeling of him, my mate.

"It'll get cold!" Charolette shouted again, her voice muffled through the closed door.

Ares stared up at me, his dark brown eyes never leaving mine. He thrust his fingers deeper inside of me, in and out, quickly and ruthlessly. "I'm not finished ruining this pretty pussy of yours, Aurora. Tonight, I'm going to fuck you until you can't walk, until your claws are digging into my back and leaving deep red marks, until your legs are trembling with nothing but pleasure."

I dug my nails into the bedsheets, slapped a hand over my mouth, and came all over his fingers, my legs shaking. My eyes rolled back, and I moaned into my palm, squirming up to the headboard and trying to make the intense pleasure rushing through me go away.

Ares growled, slapped my bare pussy one last time, and tossed me my shorts. "Get dressed before she decides to barge into the room," he said, standing up and adjusting his hardness in his gray sweatpants.

When I shimmied back into my shorts, Ares stood back and glanced down at my growing bump. He moved closer to me, swallowed hard, and stretched his large hand across the bump, unusual uncertainty in his eyes.

"That's your pup inside me," I whispered, hoping to make him smile.

And while he did, the smile didn't reach his eyes.

I wrapped my arms around his shoulders. "I know that you're nervous about how you'll lead a pack or a family without Mars, but you're going to be a great father, Ares. I know you will. You will succeed in every part of your life."

Usually, he'd give me a really alpha-hole reply, but today, he just forced another empty smile on his face and glanced down at my belly bump between us. He moved his fingers against it, my pup kicking his hand almost instinctively.

"We should get breakfast before it gets cold," he said.

I curled my hand around his bicep, still thinking about his

nightmares, and followed him through the large hallways to the kitchen. Charolette sat at the table, eating her pancakes with Marcel beside her, drawing his knuckles against hers in what looked to be a secret little touch.

Ares sat across from her, brows furrowed slightly. "Where'd you get that bruise?"

Charolette's forearm was covered in a huge brown bruise.

She pursed her lips. "That's none of your business."

"It is my business, Charolette," Ares said. "You're my sister."

"Well, maybe I like rough sex," Charolette huffed and turned back to her breakfast. "Mind your damn business. Nothing's wrong."

When Ares growled at her and her mate, Marcel glanced at Ares and me.

"She's getting worse," he said to us through the mind link, his eyes almost glazed over with tears. *"It's her cancer."*

Ares stiffened beside me. I placed my hand on his shoulder and gently rubbed it, wondering if I'd be able to heal her with my newly found power I'd discovered when I healed Elijah. Hell, I didn't even know the first thing about using it, but maybe Medusa could teach me how to use it for the better.

Charolette was dying, and I couldn't just sit back and watch the life drain from one of my best friends. Because if Charolette died too, I feared that I'd also lose Ares.

CHAPTER 4

ARES

*M*y sister couldn't die.

I refused to believe that her bruise had originated from her sickness. Hell, as much as I hated the thought, I'd prefer that Marcel had really given it to her during rough sex or whatever the fuck that excuse was.

Balling my hands into fists, I stared emptily at Mars's fucking therapist. Aurora sat next to me on the living room couch, shifting her weight from one hip to the other every few moments and making me so fucking anxious.

"How are you feeling, Ares?" Denise asked, crossing one leg over the other. Her black skirt rode up her calf enough for me to see the large bite mark in her flesh from the hound attack.

Fuck, I didn't even like this woman, yet I still felt like a shitty alpha for letting her get hurt during the battle weeks ago. She shouldn't have been in danger, Aurora shouldn't have been in danger, and *Mars* shouldn't have been in danger.

But they all had been.

And it was my fault that I couldn't save him.

"Fine," I said between clenched teeth, holding all the pain inside me.

"I've been so busy with counseling the pups that I've barely seen you. Has anything unusual happened since the last time we spoke?" she asked me.

I placed one hand on Aurora's knee and squeezed tightly. "No."

Aurora stopped shifting and pushed back her shoulders. "Yes, actually. Ares told me that Mars died, but I ... I did some research about dissociative identity disorder this past weekend and thought that personalities and alters couldn't just die." She glanced over at me with big eyes, as if to apologize. "Maybe I'm wrong, but ..."

When she suddenly got quiet, I dug my fingers into her thigh. *But ...* she wished that Mars were still alive too. Like the rest of this pack, she didn't want to believe that he had sacrificed himself for her. Yet he was gone.

And he wasn't coming back.

Denise hummed and furrowed her brows. "Mars died?" she asked me, pushing a couple strands of her silver hair out of her face with the tip of her pen, which had flown into her face from the harsh wind drifting in through the open window. "When do you think he died?"

"Don't talk down to me. He *did* die, during the hound attack. He sacrificed himself." I clenched my jaw and my fists tighter, hard enough to draw blood. "He shouldn't have fucking done it. I should've talked him the fuck out of it. He's fucking gone now."

I stared down at the bead of thick red liquid rolling down my arm. How much I could hurt myself seemed to be the only fucking thing I could control anymore. I didn't even have power over my fucking life, especially with those damn nightmares.

Denise glanced down at my palms and leaned forward, grasping my hand. "Please refrain from these self-harming behaviors here, Ares. You know how to regulate them, and I doubt Aurora wants to see this. We're trying to help you ..."

Aurora stared at me with huge, sorrowful eyes. "It's okay, Ares. I'm here for you."

My claws ached to dig into my palms further, but I forcefully unballed them.

"With your condition," Denise started, "alters don't usually just die. If he sacrificed himself, you would've died too, Ares. Mars might be in hiding, or he's merged with your alter, so you've become one man again."

I stood and towered over her. "He's gone. Dead." My blood boiled. "I felt him leave!"

She held out her hand to me. "Ares, please, calm down."

"Don't tell me to calm the fuck down," I said through gritted teeth, my nails lengthening into claws again and my canines emerging from under my lips. "You're not the one who has to deal with him being gone! You don't have to live with yourself, knowing that you couldn't protect him. How the fuck am I supposed to stay calm when I'm filled with nothing but wrath and pain, and I want to hurt fucking everyone?"

Denise held a steady gaze and gestured to the seat. "Sit down and talk to me about how you're feeling after not seeing him for over two weeks now. You must be hurting, and I want you to be able to express yourself, like Mars did with me."

"I'm fine," I said. "Fine as I can fucking be."

"Aurora told me that you're having nightmares," Denise continued.

Feeling betrayed, I growled again and sat back down next to Aurora. I didn't fucking want to be here and didn't appreciate Aurora telling this woman about my business, but I didn't want to see this lady again. I wanted this fucking thing to be over already, and I knew she wouldn't leave until I at least tried to make myself seem okay.

"She mentioned that you mumble in your sleep, that you

refuse to talk with her about what's going on. She's worried about you, Ares. She wants you to get better. She understands that Mars is gone for now and that—"

"For good," I said, glaring out the window. "Mars is gone for good."

She paused for a few moments. "So, are you telling me that you died and came back to life? Because if Mars is really dead, that is the only way that you're here, chatting with me." She rested her hands in her lap and waited for me to say something. "Is this what happened?"

"No." I seethed. "I didn't die. Mars did."

She wrote a couple things in her notebook and then placed it on the coffee table. "I don't want to fight with you, Ares. Aurora and I are just trying to understand why you think he's gone. What makes you think that Mars died?"

"I don't know what happened," I said, still angry.

"Yes, you do. Don't repress your memories. You know what happened."

Truth was that I didn't want to relive that harrowing memory.

I glanced over at Aurora, frowned, and then turned back to Denise. "Aurora will hate me," I whispered, filled with fear.

It had been bad the first time I experienced it; if I made Aurora go through it, too, she would realize how weak I truly was.

She'd think less of me.

She'd think I wasn't good enough to be a father and protect our pup. And she'd be right.

Despite my warning, Aurora rested her hand on mine and squeezed. "I won't hate you," she whispered. "I want you to be healthy, Ares. I don't want you to have nightmares every night or think that you're going through this by yourself. I'm here with you through everything."

We sat in silence for five minutes. I didn't want to talk about it, but neither of them would let me out of here without telling them what had happened. So, I suppressed the urge I had to break something when the memories came flooding back into my fragile mind.

"Mars was fighting Fenris," I finally said. "I was there; I could see it all. Fenris cut into his ribs, right over his heart, and Mars stopped breathing. Then, I came into control, and Mars wasn't alive anymore." I licked my lips and shook my head. "Mars was gone, just gone. I haven't felt him since."

Aurora squeezed my hand just a bit harder. "If what Denise is saying is true, Mars can't just be gone for good, right? Or ... maybe these are just delusions or ... I don't know ... I just want you to be okay again, Ares."

Seeing the pain on her face fucking hurt. She thought that I was making this all up, that this fucking *illness* that Denise claimed I had was forcing me to come up with ideas that couldn't be true. This was why I fucking hated that bitch.

Everyone thought that there was something wrong with me. Even my mate.

Almost as if she sensed my pain, Aurora brushed some hair out of my face. "I believe you, Ares. I just ..."

"You miss Mars," I said blankly, my heart aching. "I fucking miss him, too, but he's gone."

"No," Aurora said. "I mean, yes, I do miss him. But I want to take away your pain."

"If Fenris cut into your ribs and punctured your heart, wouldn't you have died too? Your body would be unlivable and unsustainable," Denise reasoned. "You wouldn't be breathing, let alone sitting here and talking to me. I think what you might be experiencing is separation anxiety."

"No ..." I said, refusing to let this bitch tell me what my reality looked like. "It happened."

A deafening silence fell over the room again, the wind whistling outside and shouts from practice drifting in through the open window. I should be out there, training with my pack and not talking to this fucking lady about my life.

"What was your first memory?" Denise asked me. "Not Mars's first memory. Yours."

Another thought I didn't want to relive.

"Ares?" Denise asked after I didn't answer.

"A nightmare of watching Fenris rape my mother." I balled my hands into fists and pinched my lips together. "That is the first thing that I remember in this lifetime. He shoved her onto the bed and ripped off her clothes and did fucking unspeakable things to her while I watched from the closet. When I woke up from that sleep, I refused to be as timid as Mars. I fucking vowed that I wouldn't let anyone see something like that again."

"So, you've never lived without Mars," Denise confirmed.

"No."

Mars might've known life without me, but I had never known life without Mars.

Mars had needed someone to protect him when he was younger, so I had shown up and declared myself to be his protector. I defended him every single fucking step of the way until I couldn't anymore. I'd fucking screwed up, letting him take control and die.

"And how might that first memory relate to you now?"

I might fucking hate myself, but I loathed Denise.

"Because now, I'm fucking helpless," I said between gritted teeth, letting the pain take control. "I can't do shit about it, and I can't fucking bring my other half back. I'm stuck as this man who wants to do nothing but hurt and kill, a monster that Mars would've been ashamed of."

"You're not a monster, Ares," Aurora whispered, tears in her eyes. "Don't think that."

But I had seen the look in her eyes when I told her Mars was gone. I had seen that sorrow and that pain. I had been the one to cause it because I couldn't protect Mars from the darkness that was death. Everything that had happened was because I wasn't strong enough.

I had never been truly strong enough.

And now, these nightmares I'd been having only made me loathe Fenris even more.

All I could see every night was the thought that he'd planted in my mind—I would never be a good enough mate. I would never truly be able to protect the only woman I loved. I wouldn't be a good father to our pup either.

Everything would crumble with me around.

I wished Fenris had killed me instead of Mars. I wished Mars could spend his life with his family because I wasn't a family man. I was a monster who bathed in the blood of the hounds and his enemies.

"Do you think you're experiencing these feelings and night-mares because you've been together for so long, and now, Mars is dormant inside of you?" Denise asked, giving me the fakest fucking smile I had seen.

"Mars is not dormant." I slammed my fists down on the wooden coffee table and broke it to pieces. "Mars is dead."

Desperate for someone to believe me, I grazed my fingers over my chest—where Fenris's claws had slipped into Mars's heart—pulled my shirt over my head, and pointed to a scar on my chest.

"Dead."

Large, glistening, and pink, the scar had almost healed completely already. It looked like it had happened years ago, not just weeks, but this had happened during the fight. Aurora stared at it with wide eyes and grazed her fingers over the scar.

And suddenly, the pink skin glowed a scarlet-red color.

CHAPTER 5

AURORA

"*W*hy is your scar glowing?" I whispered to Ares.

His skin shimmered red underneath my fingers, the color almost swimming inside of him like a pool of sanguine and scarlet. But this was impossible. How could this be? Had this happened before, and I just hadn't noticed it?

Ares glanced down at his chest and tensed, pecs flexing. "I told you, Mars is gone."

"Why is it red?" I repeated.

He paused for a moment. "I don't know."

"None of this makes sense. This should've killed you," I whispered.

A scar that deep—especially one that hadn't healed fully, even with his werewolf regenerative properties—meant that it was close to a fatal wound. And if Fenris had really slashed his claws right through Mars's rib cage and into his heart, Ares should've been dead too.

Wind blew our sheer white curtains into the room, catching

Ares's attention. He looked away from me and outside, the grandfather clock that Mom had inherited from her father dinging eleven times.

"Time's up, Denise. We have a meeting with the alpha," Ares said, tugging me toward the front door.

"I actually have to talk to Denise alone," I said, digging my heels into the hardwood floor to stop myself. As Ares glanced over at his therapist with a tense glare, chills ran down my back. I patted his chest. "I have to talk to her *alone.*"

"But, Kitten—"

"Please, Ares," I whispered. "It's not about you."

After staring at me for another moment, he grumbled to himself and walked to the front door. It wasn't that I didn't trust him, but I didn't want him to worry about me right now. With everything going on with him, he was easily angered *and* had been worried lately. I refused to add to his stress. Goddess forbid he wasn't able to handle the pain and turned to something worse for comfort.

I glanced at his scarred wrists and swallowed hard.

I'd never forgive myself if he turned back to cutting himself to deal with the stress of Mars being gone. Whether it was separation anxiety that he was experiencing or the actual realization that Mars was gone, Ares was already in a bad place.

Ares paused by the front door, jaw twitching. "I'm not leaving without you."

"The walk to the meeting is short," I said, giving him a reassuring smile.

A handful of alphas were meeting in our warrior building to chat about the war plans. The place was just down the block, and I had walked to it a million times since I was four. Nothing would happen, and if it did, there were at least ten other alphas and small groups of their warriors here with us.

"I know this land like the back of my hand, Ares. I'll be fine."

"Come with me, Aurora," Ares said, grasping my hand.

I pulled my hand out of his. "I will be there in a few moments. I need to talk to Denise."

"Then, I'll stay," he said.

"Alone," I repeated.

For the briefest moment, his eyes softened, and I thought I saw Mars. My whole heart warmed at the thought of him being here with us and of him listening in on our conversation. But like earlier this morning, it was my mind playing tricks.

Ares grasped my face, his thumb brushing roughly against my jaw. "You can talk to me about whatever you're feeling," he said, voice softer than it usually was, as if he was trying hard to be both Ares *and* Mars for me.

"I know," I said, my voice almost a whisper. "But I want to talk to her about it right now."

He cut his eyes to Denise and growled lowly. Then, he walked right out of the house with his hands clenched into fists by his sides. And I swore I saw blood drip from the palms of his hands and onto the doorstep right before he slammed the door.

When the door closed, Denise sighed heavily. "I have worked with Ares for over ten years now, and he has never been fond of me." She pushed some papers into her bag. "He's never been one to open up to me or to anybody. If you get him to open up to you, cherish it."

I walked back to the couch and sat, rubbing my sweaty palms together. "Do you think Mars is really gone?" I asked, still unsure about whether Ares knew for sure or if that scar was changing him somehow.

"To be honest with you, I've never worked with anyone else like Ares. I've worked with many people who have disconnects between their wolf and their human, but Ares is the only were-wolf with DID that I've seen." She grimaced and glanced out the window at Ares's departing figure through the woods. "I'm not sure if Mars is still there. I hope he is, especially with your baby on the way, but there is more to him now than his DID."

31

More than DID? What happened to him in that fight?

"And the nightmares?" I asked.

"I'd attribute it to his separation anxiety," she said. "His night-mares began when his mother died, and he fell down into a pit of self-loathing and self-harm. When we started working together, they became less frequent, but just keep an eye on him, as I know that you don't want that to happen again."

My stomach tightened, and I tried hard to think about all the good times. I had never seen Ares hurt himself—maybe refuse to help himself, but not hurt himself willingly. Part of me didn't believe that he would do such a thing, and the other part of me feared that this would be the end of him.

I nervously ran my fingers across the suede couch and gnawed on the inside of my lip. "I actually called you over for more than just Ares and his nightmares. Since Elijah placed the second half of the stone into my back, I've been feeling different."

Denise tucked some silver hair behind her ear. "Different how?"

"Powers and … memories that aren't my own."

The memories weren't bad *yet*. I had only remembered the good things, but by the way Helios had tensed at Nyx's name during the hound fight, I knew that I was on the cusp of having vivid nightmares about Nyx and Helios.

"What kind of memories?"

"Memories about these gods," I whispered, a chill washing over me. "I don't know what to make of them. People keep calling me Dawn and acting as if I know them, but I don't remember who they are. I want to remember. I just can't. In these memories, I'm friends with gods and goddesses. It is almost like I am one myself."

The memories had seemed to be of hundreds of years ago, yet Helios was still alive and well today. What if this Nyx and Dawn were still alive too? Were they fighting for peace in the underworld?

"And you said that they started the night after the hound attack?"

"Yes. I haven't said anything to anyone because I don't want Ares to worry about me."

I stared out the window, lost in my thoughts and drifting into another memory of the past.

CRADLING a rogue's snout in my hand, I drew my fingers across his fur and rested my forehead against his. Helios's flaming chariot was perched a few yards away from me in the moonflower meadow, the heat from the fire hitting me in thick, suffocating waves.

A branch broke from my left, and Nyx appeared in the woods, her skin glowing. When I saw her, I mumbled some Latin words to the rogue and stood, skipping over to Nyx and looping my arm around hers.

"Where have you been?" I asked. "I've been waiting for you."

Her lips curled into a smile almost immediately. "Enjoying the dawn."

If I remembered anything from my dream last night, it was that Nyx had probably been with Helios somewhere in these woods, spending the dawn with him in secrecy because nobody could know about their relationship, for some ungodly reason.

I pulled Nyx over to the rogues and picked up a crown of glowing white moonflowers that I had made earlier that morning. "This is for you," I said, fixing it on her head and biting my bottom lip. "It looks so good on you! I know these flowers don't survive in the underworld, but I thought it'd be cute for you to wear while you're here. You're always complaining that Erebus doesn't let you bring any underworld jewelry here."

Helios walked out from the woods, his eyes flickering to us. "Good morning, Dawn."

I glanced over at him, brow arched. "Not going to say good morning to Nyx too?"

"She's had a good morning already," Helios said, climbing into his

33

chariot and hanging over the edge with that goofy smile on his face and a lightness in his eyes that told me there was some double meaning behind his comment.

I scrunched up my nose and waved him off. "It's too early for your dirty comments about my best friend. I'll see you tomorrow."

After glancing over at Nyx, Helios pulled on his horses' reins. They took off into the air, lighting up the morning sky with flaming light. Nyx stared at him and smiled, so much love in her eyes. And I couldn't fathom why she couldn't be with him openly.

Why does it have to be a secret?

I gently nudged her shoulder, wanting more information. "What's going on with you and my brother?" I asked with innocence in my voice, so she'd trust me. If this was a memory, I didn't want to taint it. But if this was something else ... I didn't want Nyx to become suspicious of me.

Gods in the underworld were known to be evil, selfish, and savage monsters. That was what I had gathered from the hound attack, but Nyx seemed a bit too sweet. These memories didn't make much sense to me.

Nyx stared emptily at the disintegrated grass where Helios's flaming chariot had once been parked. Pain and anguish and ... anger washed over her expression, chilling me right down to my core.

I waved my hand in front of her gaze. "Hello? Are you daydreaming about him now?" I wrinkled my nose when she still hadn't answered me, not wanting even the ghost of her to catch on to me watching this intimate memory, and sat. "You know what? I don't even want to know."

Nyx sat down beside me. "No, I wasn't."

Lie.

She was lying.

I could see it on her face.

Cheeks flushed, she rolled onto her stomach and sniffed the moonflowers in the meadow, inhaling the scent of wolves and rogues who had probably lain by my side last night. She kicked her legs back and forth and smiled to herself.

The rogue wolf from earlier rested his head in my lap. I stroked its fur and wondered why Nyx had asked me about taming the hounds in my last memory. Hounds lived in the underworld and were controlled by Fenris.

How could I tame them?

"Oh, come on," I found myself saying in the memory, my icy-white hair blowing in the breeze. "You know that I know about you two. I hide you two. I can see it in Helios's eyes every time I mention your name. Is it still just flirting, or is there more?"

"Dawn," Nyx said, voice suddenly sharp. "Please, not now."

"Fine. I'll tell you about my love life whether you want to hear about it or not," I said, my gaze focused on her. "As long as you promise that you won't tell anyone."

"You know me, Dawn." Nyx smiled at me. "I wouldn't do that."

"Well, you know, Ares has been trying to get with me forever. And oh my gosh! I finally decided to give him a shot again. We spent the entire day last week just staring up at the sky and clouds, and then I got him to watch the wolves run during the dusk with me!"

"Did you guys ..." Nyx asked, raising her brows.

My cheeks flushed as I thought about Ares, and I stuffed my face into my hands. "He was amazing in bed," I said, fanning myself. "Same as he has been for thousands of years. Between him and Mars, I have my hands full."

"I totally forgot you'd gotten with him before," Nyx said. "Why'd you guys part ways?"

"Hella," I found myself saying, the goddess's name coming off my lips like daggers. "Hella has a thing for him. He doesn't like her back. I didn't want to get into the drama back then. He stayed away to protect me." I paused for the slightest moment. "I'm afraid she's going to start acting crazy again. She's killed mortals who've claimed to have slept with him before ..." Glancing down at the wolf in my lap, I swallowed hard. "And the wolves have been getting rowdier lately, as if they can sense their hound relatives in the underworld."

"Dawn, you know that I'd do anything to protect you from her," Nyx said, grasping my hands tightly and giving me a huge smile. She

was too nice for a god of the underworld and didn't belong there.
"Anything."

"Aurora?" Denise said, brows pinched together. "Are you still with me?"

I shook my head and pulled myself out of my mind, wrapping my arms around my body and hoping to rid myself of these thoughts that felt so real. They seemed so close to reality that I could almost catch them within my grasp.

"Sorry," I said, tucking some hair behind my ear. "The memories are becoming more vivid and happening more often. I can't find a trigger for them. They seem to come and go as they please."

"Similar to Ares, do you think maybe"—she let out another heavy breath—"you're using these memories to process the disappearance of your mate? When some wolves lose their mate, they do experience nightmares."

Denise was going the logical, sensical route. And while I was all for science, sometimes, the supernatural overcame all truth and proved to be the scariest fucking thing in this world.

She might attribute this to losing Mars, but to me, this could mean only one thing.

This stone inside me had been in someone before me, someone named Dawn, who was a soft woman and befriended gods as powerful as Helios, the god of the sun, and Nyx, the goddess of the night.

Little did I know that these dreams were nothing but a web that Nyx had woven for me, an end that would destroy my life if I wasn't careful, and a destruction so powerful that it had split a single man in two.

CHAPTER 6

ARES

I sat at the head of the table, glaring down the other alphas and waiting not-so-patiently for Aurora, so we could start this fucking meeting already. After the hound attack and these nightmares that had been plaguing my mind, I hated the thought of leaving Aurora alone.

What if something happened and I wasn't there to stop it?

My claws cut into my palms again. Something *had* happened while I was around, and I still couldn't stop it. What would I do to protect Aurora? With the Malavite Stone, Aurora was now stronger than I was. How could her lousy man and mate do *anything*?

I couldn't.

I fucking couldn't.

Some of the alphas mumbled to their betas, and I cut my gaze to them. Fuming.

Why had Aurora stayed back? What did she need to talk to Denise about? Denise might've helped Mars, but I didn't trust her, especially now that Mars was gone. She had always favored him, always treated him differently than she treated me. She talked down to me like she knew more than I ever could.

Balling my hands into fists even harder, I sighed as the blood leaked from my palms and enjoyed the pain a bit too much. But I fucking deserved all the agony in the world for ever letting Mars sacrifice himself, for letting him leave Aurora with me.

Alone, I wasn't good for her. I'd hurt her. *I hurt everyone.*

"What are we waiting for?" Alpha Pax asked. He was one of the many alphas who hadn't come to the last meeting, thinking that I wasn't trustworthy enough, one who could've helped stopped this fucking chaos before it ever started.

But it was too late for that shit.

When the door swung open, Aurora hurried into the room with Ruffles standing by her side. "Sorry I'm late," Aurora said, her sweet scent drifting in through my nostrils and making me unclench my fists. She sat next to me and smiled at the other alphas. "What did I miss?"

"Nothing," I said, letting my palm heal before she could see it.

"Well then, let's start," Aurora said, addressing the room. "We have hound problems."

"They're tearing up the Sanguine Wilds and getting stronger by the day," I continued. "And they aren't hellhounds, like we originally thought. A necromancer from the underworld is turning dead wolves into undead monsters who want to kill us all."

"And where are these hounds now?" Pax asked, brows raised. Or maybe he just didn't fucking want to be here. He strived for peace, but peace wasn't an option when dealing with hounds. "The forest has been silent these past couple weeks."

"They're in the underworld, fighting gods," Aurora said, tucking a strand of her long brown hair behind her ear.

A fire flashed through her eyes, and I growled at the thought of her thinking about Helios—that god who seemed to know and care for her almost too much.

"I think we should bring the fight to them," Alpha Vulcan said stoically, shaking his head of dark red hair. "I saw the destruction they can do. They kill ruthlessly, and I don't want any of my people—or *any* alpha's people—to be killed."

"I agree," Minerva said. "I visited Alpha Ares's old pack, and everything was destroyed."

Ruffles placed two paws on the table and looked at me. "*Meow*," she said in agreement.

"You suggest we go to the underworld?" Alpha Olen said, skeptical. Like the rest of these assholes, that old man never quite liked me. "How do you suggest we get there? The only path to the underworld as mortals is death, and we can't fight when we're dead."

"I might have an idea," Aurora said, gnawing on the inside of her lip.

Everyone looked over at her, including Ruffles, who could almost sense what was going to come out of Aurora's mouth because she growled lowly.

Aurora petted her gray fur to calm her down. "Medusa—"

"Medusa?" Pax said, chuckling. "She's a myt—"

I grabbed his collar, thrust him against the table, and growled, "Don't interrupt my mate."

Everyone tensed, and I let my claws break right through the cloth of his shirt. When Aurora placed her hand on my thigh, I released him and sat back.

"Let her finish," I said. "She knows more about this than you do."

Pax sat back and huffed, readjusting himself.

"Medusa isn't a myth," Aurora continued. "We've met her more than once, and we have seen what she can do. The stories of her turning people to stone are true." Her voice wavered slightly, as if she didn't know if the next part of her sentence would come off as crazy. "Those people must go somewhere. They were in the midst of a battle with hounds. What if they went to the underworld when she turned them to stone?"

"You're saying that Medusa could get us to the underworld alive? That when she turns people to stone, it doesn't kill them?" Pax asked, tilting his head at Aurora as if he didn't believe her. "I don't believe in an unpeaceful witch like her."

Vulcan cleared his throat. "Aurora is telling the truth."

"It could work," Minerva agreed.

Pax laughed lifelessly and stood up, capturing the attention of the other alphas. "Are we seriously going to trust that Medusa would ever help a bunch of werewolves get to the underworld in one piece? Who knows what's down there? We could get stuck there if we're not careful."

I stood to meet his intense stare. "Sounds like you're fucking scared."

This guy kept pissing me off. He fucking deserved to be belittled.

"My pack would have wiped out all those hounds by now, Ares," he said to me, eyes shifting from green to gold.

If he wanted a fight, I would fucking give him one. Right here, right now.

Pax growled, "I'm not afraid of the underworld, but it seems like *you* are."

"You would've been shitting your pants if you had seen what we did," Vulcan said to him.

Minerva rolled her brown eyes and leaned closer to Aurora. "What did I tell you? Testosterone will get us all killed one day. Take care of this," she said, tapping her fingers on the wooden table, "before I have to."

Pressing her fingertips into the long wooden table until they turned white, Aurora stood. "This is not the time for arguments. We're fighting for our lives. Those hounds don't care who you are. They will kill children, pups, elders, anyone. None of us are safe, which is why we need to bring the fight to them."

There was a fire in her voice, a strength that I had only seen during the hound attack. Aurora had grown so much since the day Mars and I had met her at the lake. She had become more than a woman and much more than a luna. Aurora had become an alpha who inspired.

"I'm not sure if it'll work," Aurora continued, glancing from alpha to alpha. "But I will find out what I can from Medusa and get back to everyone."

Everyone at the table must've felt the power radiating off her because even the chattiest of alphas fell silent and became tense. Aurora wasn't to be questioned this time. Her mother might've never believed in her, but these other alphas did.

"Everyone should prepare for war, whether you go to the underworld with us or not."

Again, a heavy silence fell upon the group of alphas. With so much pride, I stared at my mate, a woman who was able to command an entire room of egotistical assholes, and found myself thinking of how much more she deserved.

This woman had power close to a goddess's now. Even Helios had recognized it.

After a few long moments of silence, Olen finally nodded. "I plan to go to the underworld with you, Aurora. My warriors are some of the strongest in the Sanguine Wilds. We will destroy anyone who threatens our peace."

"I'll go too," another alpha said. "My ancestors fought in the War of the Lycans. My pack will honor them."

"Mine too," another said.

When the room erupted into an argument about which pack would descend into the underworld and which alpha had the strongest warriors, Aurora glanced over at me and smiled, her hand traveling across her bump.

"We're going to create a better future for our pup," she said. "We're not alone anymore."

"We're going to *fight* for a better future, Aurora. Nothing is certain."

But, hell, I'd try my hardest to make it happen.

CHAPTER 7

AURORA

"*D*o you think Medusa can do it?" I asked Ares after all the other alphas filed out of the meeting room.

Ruffles sat in the chair beside him, furiously licking her back after one of the alphas petted her the wrong way.

I nervously stared out the large glass window and rubbed my hands together. "I don't know the extent of her power."

And ... Pax was right.

We didn't know what was down in the underworld. Medusa had told us that horrid things happened to those people in stone and that some of them didn't come back. How would Ares and I go down to the underworld to fight when we had a baby we needed to raise? Our little girl would be in so much danger—and even more so if Hella found out about our pup. Hella might try to kill her.

I shook my head to get rid of the thought.

We'd eliminate Hella before she ever had the chance of hurting anyone in our family or in our pack again. I didn't care

43

what we had to do; we would do it to protect our family and our home from the monsters and gods like her.

Ares slapped the wooden table with his palm. "Sit up here and talk to me."

After arching a brow, I hesitantly jumped up onto the table, kicked off my shoes, and rested my feet on his thighs, my mind still reeling with hesitant thoughts. Whether I was pregnant or not, Ares and I had to go down to the underworld. Out of everyone here, we knew the most about these hounds, and we were the strongest wolves to grace this land.

While I wasn't quite sure what that scar on his chest meant, the Malavite Stone swayed with power in my back. If I didn't go, every one of those alphas, their warriors, and their packs would die from hound attacks.

Ares rested his large hands on my knees and rubbed them gently. "You're worried."

I stared down at his sculpted face and brushed my fingers over his chiseled jaw, my heart. "We don't know what lies in the underworld," I said. "For all we know, we could be putting ourselves into more danger."

"Hmm," Ares said, trailing his fingers up the inside of my thigh and under my skirt, disappearing inside my panties. "What else do you have on your mind, Kitten? Let me help you relax a bit."

"Ares," I said, glancing over to my left at the large window that anyone could look right into and see what we were doing. "Can you not do this right now? This is serious."

Ares rubbed two fingers against my clit. "I'm listening."

"What if someone comes in?"

"They'll see me fucking my mate, and I'll have to kill them for it," he said as if it were no big deal, as if he would just kill someone for *me*. He slipped two fingers inside of me, and I squeezed him. "You're so tight for me. Does that make my kitten excited, seeing her mate defend her honor?"

I pressed my lips together, feeling his fingers thrust in and out of me. "I ... we need to talk about this right now," I whispered, trying to think straight. But his fingers were so long and rough and big that I couldn't quite think about anything other than his promise to me earlier—that he'd fuck me today.

"I'm listening," Ares repeated, staring up at me with golden eyes, his lips parted slightly.

My pussy clenched, and I closed my eyes for a brief moment, fingers curling around the edge of the wooden table. "If we need to go ... to the underworld, we need to go ... talk to ... Medusa."

"We will." He curled his fingers right over my G-spot, hitting me at just the right angle.

I tightened more and took a deep breath to try to hold back my moans.

He grasped my jaw in his other hand, his thumb massaging my clit. "We'll go tonight. Or will you be too sore to move after I fuck you?"

I parted my lips slightly, desperate to form coherent words.

"Lost for words, Kitten? Do my fingers feel that good inside of you?"

Ruffles took one glance at us, scrunched up her nose, and walked out of the room, her little butt swaying back and forth. She pushed the door closed behind her with her paw, leaving me alone with my beast.

Barely able to hold myself together, I pursed my lips and nodded.

"Are you going to purr for me when I shove my cock inside of this snug pussy?" Ares asked, taking my pussy lips between his two fingers and squeezing gently.

My core tensed even more, and I nodded yet again, knowing that my mouth would betray me if I opened it. I could just feel the moan in my throat, waiting to come out the second that I parted my lips.

"Use your words," Ares commanded, golden eyes glowing even more intense by the second.

He massaged my G-spot with his two fingers, and I tensed up at the feeling. So close ... I was so fucking close.

"Yes," I whispered.

He curled his fingers one last time inside of me, and I moaned, unable to hold it back.

After he pulled his fingers out of me, he stood and stuffed them into my mouth. "Tell me how your sweet cunt tastes on my fingers," he said, unzipping his jeans with his other hand.

When he tugged me to the edge of the table, I gasped. Ares just stuffed his fingers deeper inside my mouth until they nearly hit the back of my throat.

"Suck off all your juices, Kitten. Be a good girl for me, and you'll be rewarded."

I wrapped my lips around his fingers, sucked myself off him, and closed my eyes, moaning at the taste. Ares slowly pulled them out of me and unleashed his cock from his briefs, pushing his head against my sopping wet entrance.

"Do you want your reward?" he asked, rubbing his hard dick in his hand against my clit. "Hmm? Do you want to feel good, Aurora?"

"Yes, please," I whispered, clenching.

"You've made me wait all day for this pussy. The least you can do is beg for my cock."

Glancing down between us, I whimpered at the sight of pre-cum Ares was brushing against me. Covered in glistening juices, the head of his cock moved back and forth against my clit, making me desperate.

"Give it to me," I begged.

"Oh, Kitten, you have better manners than that."

"Please, Alpha. Give me your big, fat co—"

Ares pushed himself inside of me, seizing my hips and pumping furiously. The pressure rose in my core, his lips capturing mine. I curled my fingers into his chest, watching his scar glow an even brighter red, and found myself remembering something so faint, so distant that I almost didn't think it was real.

My fingers had been curled into his chest with this sanguine-colored scar before, his thick muscle under my fingertips. He'd had his arms around me, holding me tightly to his bloodied chest and whispering about slaughtering *anyone* who came close to us.

"I'll pierce my spear right through their hearts for you, Kitten," he had murmured in my mind. *"Only for you."*

"Ares," I cried, coming closer to the edge of a blissful orgasm.

"Come for me," he murmured into my ear.

I threw my head back slightly, still in that long-forgotten memory, and moaned softly as the god of war destroyed all our enemies with a bloody spear and his savage, bare hands.

CHAPTER 8

AURORA

*A*res and I ran through the deserted land of Hound Territory toward Medusa's house, which sat on a single plateau on the terrifying, jagged Syncome Mountains range. Since I could run—and run faster than a normal wolf—now, we made it there in record time, without stumbling upon any fog or any hounds.

We shifted into our human form and walked up the dirt path lined with statues of gods and goddesses. And this time, I could only wonder if these were really just statues or real people who Medusa had turned to stone.

"This place always makes me nervous," I whispered to Ares, glancing around at the bare mountain that held no signs of life or vegetation. Yet down below, on the opposite side of the mountain, monstrous growls echoed from a dark forest, shielded by thick leaves and greenery.

"We're almost there, Kitten," Ares said, the setting sunlight hitting the side of his face.

He looked so stoic, so divine and godlike here.

The memory from earlier still plagued my mind, and I couldn't seem to shake the thought of being together with Ares in another life. Maybe he hadn't been Ares, or maybe he really had been. I didn't know for sure. All that was certain was that I had touched him before, we had been together, and I had loved him.

My lips curled into a smile, warmth spreading through my chest.

Ares and I were meant to be. In every lifetime.

"You gonna keep walking?" Ares asked from behind me. He stood at Medusa's front door with a smug smirk on his face and his big arms crossed over his chest while watching me completely miss Medusa's home and continue on the pathway. I was just so lost in my thoughts. "Daydreaming too much about me, Aurora?"

With my cheeks flushing, I narrowed my eyes at him and walked back toward her small centuries-old house built into a jagged peak. Like last time, her dirty white curtains blew outward through her windows.

After knocking without an answer three times, I opened her front door and stepped into the house. "Medusa?" I called, hoping that she was home and maybe just sleeping.

We barged in without her permission, but I was worried about her. I hadn't heard from her since the hound attack and since the loud boom that had echoed throughout the forest and turned everyone to stone; everyone except her.

No answer.

"Come on," I said to Ares, holding the door open for him. "We should see if we can figure out where she went off to. If we're going to the underworld, we need to find her as soon as possible. She had to have left something lying around."

I drew my fingers across the ancient walls and glanced around her house, desperate to find any trace of her and where she could've gone. Had she ever even come back here since that chaotic battle?

Looking through every room, I wanted to find something—an unclean dish, dirty clothes, a note about where she might've been all this time. But instead, I found nothing out of the ordinary and nothing to signal she had been back here.

As Ares looked through her bedroom, I walked into the living room and found a journal on her coffee table with a slip of paper pushed between a couple loose pages. After opening it to that page, I sat down on the couch and read through the notebook.

I shouldn't have, but it was important for me to understand Medusa. Something drew me to her, and I couldn't really put my finger on it. Not only did I want to get to know her, but I also felt the *need* to get to know her more than I ever wanted to know anyone.

Maybe it was because she just had so much knowledge about this war and the hounds.

The notebook was filled with useless scribbles and some words in Latin that I both had trouble understanding yet could grasp parts of it, even without any training in the Latin language. The journal dated back to over two hundred years ago during the War of the Lycans, when it was said that werewolves had gone to war with the hounds.

1752 May 2

Dawn is dead. Helios went to the underworld to fight for her honor. He will die down there too, I suppose. I'd warned him not to go. I told him the consequences. I told him Hella is out to destroy the Sanguine Wilds, but that stubborn god hadn't listened to me. They never do.

Selene has gathered wolves, both warriors and rogues, to fight the hounds when they appear. The army of hounds have disappeared from the Sanguine Wilds for two weeks now, and not one lone hound has been spotted in this forest for weeks. But they're coming back. I feel it.

We must prepare for a war and for the first goddess to be reborn. If we don't, this war will never end. We'll be trapped in this hell forever.

MY HEART POUNDED as I read the passage, my Latin getting better with each word. I swallowed hard, afraid to read what was on the next page, but I couldn't help myself from turning the thick, delicate paper and taking it all in. It made little sense out of context, but Helios and Hella were both mentioned, which gave me some understanding.

1752 MAY 15

The hounds came flooding into the Sanguine Wilds. Resurrected as a hound, even Dawn came, viciously killing the rogues who had once loved her. I'm afraid the gods won't survive this. They are weaker by the day.

TWO WEEKS … two weeks since the initial entry, the hounds had attacked again.

My stomach twisted into knots. This sounded exactly like what we were going through now. Two weeks had already passed, just like in her passage, which meant we had two more weeks at the most before the hounds came back to slaughter us.

Was time repeating? Or was the War of the Lycans still happening?

1797 JUNE 8

The warriors have pushed the hounds back into the underworld. Helios came back for the briefest moment with some old warriors, not having aged a day down there. This war is far from over. I'm afraid for the future of humanity.

. . .

IT HAD TAKEN the warriors over forty years to push the hounds back into the underworld once they came here. I rested my hand over my bump, my heart racing. I couldn't let that happen. My girl wasn't going to be raised in a living hell. We needed to get to the underworld as soon as possible.

1923 JANUARY 11

Nobody has come back. Statues have fallen. I fear the worst is yet to come.

AND THEN THE PASSAGES ENDED.

I stared down at the journal with wide eyes, my hand over my growing bump. "If we don't handle this now, we're all going to die," I whispered to myself.

We didn't have much time left, especially if the hounds and gods reacted the same way they had over two centuries ago.

Closing the journal, I pulled out the loose page and glanced at the distinct handwriting and charred page edges. This hadn't been written by Medusa, but to Medusa by ... Helios, the god of the sun.

MEDUSA,

You were right about everything.

Nyx killed Dawn.

She lured me down to the underworld while I sought revenge. She told me that the rogues and hounds who had loved and lain with Dawn tore her body to pieces. She hoped I'd never found out that she was the real woman who had done it.

But I did.

Gods and ghouls whispered about the day a goddess fell. Nyx had locked Dawn in the torture chambers, where they had chains strong enough to tether any god to the pits of the underworld, and slashed her to pieces while Hella and Erebus, Nyx's bastard brother, watched.

I should've listened to you.

One night, she bound me to those chains and tortured me in front of her brother until I was bleeding and bruised. I couldn't even use my power to get away. And when Erebus disappeared into their palace, she snuck down into my chamber and helped me escape, so I might be her secret.

When I first descended into the underworld, I played right into Nyx's hand. She had killed my sister for one sole purpose—for me to live in the underworld with her and become her secret affair at night while her brother forced himself on her during the days.

She lied to me and told me that she was doing this all for me. I put on a show and acted like I trusted her, but since you'd warned me about her evil ways, I have been going over every interaction with her endlessly.

Nyx, goddess of the night, had never been friends with Dawn. She'd used her to get closer to me.

That night, I asked her if she killed my sister. She sweated at the mere question and my intensity, but she had never sweated around me before, no matter how brightly I burned for her. That was how I knew she was lying straight through her teeth.

She pulled me through the palace, unseen, and made a run for the Styx River. It was there that I tried drowning the love of my life, but I am such a weak man. I couldn't use my entire power down in the underworld.

But I was able to escape her wrath, nearly unscathed.

If anyone desires to come down to the underworld, advise them against it. They do not want to meet the woman I once called my darkness. She is selfish. She is crazy. She is like everyone else in the underworld.

We are barely surviving down here, but we're fighting for the greater good.

I hope to meet you again one day, and I sincerely apologize for not listening to your advice. You're the wisest woman that I know, and I believe you can be one to change this world for the better.

Sincerely,

Helios

MY HANDS TREMBLED as I folded the letter and slipped it back into the notebook. No wonder I'd had a bad fucking feeling about Nyx in those memories. She wasn't a friend at all, but a deceitful liar.

"What'd the journal say?" Ares asked.

I leaped up at the sound of his voice, startled. Ares stood at the doorway, hands on his hips, glancing around the room and analyzing every single piece of ancient text.

"That we need to get to the underworld before the hounds return to the Sanguine Wilds."

Helios might've advised us against it, but I refused to let the hounds get away with this. I wanted payback for the slaughter of Mom's pack and the death of my brother—both times. These hounds were after *me* because of the stone, not these other gods. I would not let them fight for me without aiding in any way that I could.

And I certainly wouldn't let them come back to the Sanguine Wilds and hurt my daughter's chance at a secure, peaceful upbringing.

There was no exception. We had to go to the underworld, no matter what.

"We have to do this for our baby," I said, standing up and placing the journal back on the living room table, wanting to take it but knowing that Medusa would find out it was stolen if she ever came back. "We have to do anything for her. She's not going to grow up in a place like the one in this journal."

She wasn't even born yet, but I'd do anything to keep her safe.

Anything.

Though I wished that I could piece those dream memories together to figure out why Nyx and Hella had wanted me dead in the first place. Why kill me when Nyx had a joyous life in the underworld and a lover on earth? What did I have to do with any of this?

Ares moved closer to me, placed his hands on either side of my face, and kissed my forehead, not saying two more words to me. His entire body was rigid against mine, his kiss not as passionate as it had been weeks ago, before Mars died.

But I didn't say anything to him about it.

He was already in pain.

When he pulled away, I scribbled a note on a blank piece of paper, telling Medusa to come find us as quickly as she could. We had business to discuss and plans to make. We were going to destroy the hounds before they had a chance to destroy us.

CHAPTER 9

ARES

*A*fter Aurora shifted into her wolf without a problem, we ran down the jagged Syncome Mountains and through the eerily quiet hound lands. Being able to run freely through miles of land and not worrying about monsters attacking us was both fucking blissful and terrifying.

For the first time in years, the foggy sky had cleared, and the sun shimmered through the trees. Leaves had fallen off branches and decorated our path, crunching under our paws. We passed a field of moonflowers that I hadn't even known about and paused on the outskirts of it because Aurora had suddenly stopped.

She walked into the field and shifted into her human, strolling around as if she was looking for or remembering something. Brown hair blowing back in the breeze, Aurora glanced over her shoulder and smiled.

I shifted into my human form and followed her, uneasy that she wandered so freely in Hound Territory. Usually, Aurora feared hounds more than I feared losing her. How could she just walk through an untouched plot of land? It seemed like a trap.

"Where are you going?" I asked her, looking up at the setting sun. It would be dark soon, and I didn't want to have to fucking fight off a bunch of rogues on our way back to the pack house. "We should get back to the pack before the rogues come out."

"I've been here before," she whispered.

I followed after her, grasping her hand and stopping her. "This is Hound Territory."

How had she been here before? She wouldn't set foot here alone.

She brushed her fingers against the flower petals. "With Helios."

Tightening my grip around her wrist, I growled, "Helios?"

Eyes widening, Aurora slapped a hand against her mouth and tensed. "Sorry," she whispered. "I didn't mean to say that out loud. I know how much you don't like him. I just … I haven't been here with him as myself, but I can feel his presence here."

Still, Aurora had awoken the beast in me that I'd badly tried to suppress since Mars had died. I wanted to be both Ares and Mars for Aurora and had tried so desperately to shield my arrogant, asshole side of myself from her since then.

"What is he to you?" I asked through clenched teeth.

After running her hands across my chest, she looked up at me, her mate and the one man who was supposed to mean everything to her. Hearing another man's name on her lips infuriated me.

"Nothing in this life. You're everything to me, and I'm forever yours," she whispered.

"But you know him," I said, my blood boiling. "You told me you didn't."

Aurora furrowed her brows at me and frowned. "I don't know Helios, but I … I have this unexplainable feeling that I have been with him in this very spot. Let me prove it to you … somehow …"

She grasped my hand and hurried to the other side of the

field, dropping to her knees and searching the tall grass for something. She crawled around a patch of grass, dirtying her knees and covering her hair in mosquitoes from the grass.

A moment later, she popped back up with a horseshoe in her hand. "Helios rides those flaming horses. He used to park his cart in this very spot. Here's a horseshoe to prove it. I'm not crazy ..." she whispered the last part to herself. "These are real memories."

"What do you mean, real memories?" I asked her.

Snapping her head up, she swallowed hard and smiled. "I believe you."

"What?" I asked.

"I believe what you told your therapist earlier—that Mars is gone. She told you that it was just some sort of separation anxiety, but this"—she held up the horseshoe—"proves that not everything can be explained by science."

"Aurora, Kitten"—I took her face in my hands—"we need to get back home."

I didn't know what she was saying anymore. She was talking in circles.

Aurora dug her fingers into my shoulders and grinned. "It doesn't matter what happened in the past or in past lives. What matters right now is you and me. We have to kill those hounds and secure a safe future for our pup."

There it was again.

Our pup.

I sprawled my hand across her stomach, and our baby kicked damn hard. She felt as strong as me, as vicious as me too. And still, all I could feel was guilt. I wanted to be happy—I really fucking did. But Mars wasn't here. I couldn't be happy, no matter how hard I tried.

"You and me," I whispered, cracking a half-crooked smile, "and her."

"And her."

When she repeated the words, I found myself wanting to

throw up my fucking lunch. I couldn't keep lying to Aurora like this and have her keep believing that I was cut out to be a father. I couldn't fucking do it. I grasped her hard and pushed back a sea of tears that threatened to fall.

"I'm not going to be a good father," I said. "Mars would have been a good father, but I won't."

"What are you talking about?" she asked with wide eyes, taking my face in her hands and tearing up. "What are you saying? Where is this coming from?"

"I hurt people, Aurora. I don't care for them. I don't know how to love."

"You love me, don't you?" she whispered, worry etched into every fucking millimeter of her beautiful face. "Tell me you love me, Ares."

I stared down at her hands and pressed my lips together to stop them from trembling. "I love you more than you even know," I whispered, gently grasping her hand and stroking my thumb over hers.

"You care for me. You protect me. You are more than enough, Ares."

"But Mars—"

"Mars isn't here. He's gone for now. It's just me and you," she said, poking a hard finger against my chest. "So, don't think that you won't be a great father to our pup. I have seen the way that *you* interact with the pups in the pack. You care about them, even the ones from my old pack. You would do everything in your power to protect them, just like you did everything in your power to protect Mars."

With strands of brown hair blowing into her face, she stood on her toes and kissed me, her lips moving softly and slowly against mine. Wanting to feel fucking loved, I wrapped my arms around her waist and kissed her back.

My lips moved up and down the column of her neck, pressing hard enough to make her skin a light pink in the place of my lips.

I roamed my hands around her smaller body and seized her hips, picking her up and placing her in the field.

The moonflowers illuminated around us, twinkling and flickering against our flesh.

And I found myself letting go.

In some fucked up way, this was the only time I could. I hated talking about my feelings. I hated admitting my faults. I hated thinking that I would never be a good enough father to our pup.

Months ago, I'd wanted to put a pup inside of Aurora so badly.

Now, with my nightmares ... I didn't even want to think about it.

I drew my canines up the column of her neck, making her shiver, and moved my fingers against her panties. While I didn't know how to express my feelings, I damn well knew how to make my mate feel good.

"You're mine," I murmured against my mark. "Mine."

"Here, Ares?" she whispered, a moan slipping from her mouth. "We're out in the open."

Wrapping a hand around the front of her throat, I gently stroked it and gazed down into her eyes, illuminated by the flowers around us. "I'm not leaving until I get every piece of you again, Kitten." I trailed my lips down her body, grabbed her hip in my free hand, and pulled her closer to me.

Truth was that I didn't want her to pry anymore.

I hated feeling like shit.

So, I kissed up her thighs and then between her legs, leaving sloppy kisses all over her wet cunt. She sprawled her arms out around us and dug her claws into the dirt, another sweet moan escaping her lips.

Massaging her clit with my tongue, I drew my fingers against her tense inner thighs. "Stop worrying, Kitten. Nobody is going to spot us. And if they do, I'll snap their necks for you, kill them in cold blood."

Her pussy tightened, and she whimpered, lacing her hand through my thick brown hair and pulling my face closer to her core. She moved her hips against my face, back and forth, desperate to hit just the right angle.

While she did, I pushed a long finger into her pussy and growled against her clit, making it vibrate.

She tossed her head back again and pulled my hair harder. "Oh my Goddess, Ares. More!"

"More, Kitten?" I asked. "You want more?"

"More, please, Alpha."

After picking her up, I twirled her around and set her on her hands and knees in the middle of the moonflower field. With her back against my chest, I positioned my cock at her entrance and buried my face into the crook of her neck.

"I love you," I mumbled into her ear, tugging on her nipple.

She whimpered and clenched against the head of my cock.

Goddess, I loved those sexy moans of hers.

Grasping her hip in one hand and her swollen breast in the other, I pushed the head of my dick into her aching cunt. She bit her lip, entire body tense, and pushed back against me, my desperate kitten letting out a purr when her ass met my hips.

She stiffened around me, squeezing my dick harder than she ever had, and moved herself on my length. I leaned over her, taking both her tits in my hands and squeezing gently, her nipples rolling against my palms and making my cock even harder.

"Back and forth on me, Kitten," I murmured into her ear, sliding my fingers to her hardened nipples and tugging until she whimpered again. "Just like that. Keep moving on your alpha's dick. Your pussy is just swallowing up my cock."

After digging her claws even further into the dirt, Aurora bounced faster and faster, her tits swaying wildly underneath her and in my palms. If she kept this up for much longer, I was going to fucking fill her snug pussy with my entire load.

I gently bit down on her mark and sucked it between my teeth. "It feels good, doesn't it?"

She nodded, her pussy pulsing around the base of my cock. "More, Alpha. I can't move any faster. I want you to pound me into—"

Before she could finish her sentence, I seized her breasts and used her body to thrust my cock in and out of her pussy, destroying it as quickly as I could. I slipped some of my fingers from her tit to her pussy and rubbed torturous circles around her clit. She closed her eyes, clenching hard around me, and wiggled in my grasp.

When my balls smacked against her clit, too, she tossed her head back and screamed out, her pussy clamping down on my dick and sucking the cum right out of it. I grunted—nothing felt better than this—and fell back in the field with her still in my arms.

Wanting to get every last drop inside her, I moved my hips up and down, ramming my cock into her. She squeezed me even more when I sucked on my mark on her neck and growled into her ear, making sure Aurora knew who she belonged to.

With my dick still buried balls deep inside her, I lay against the field and wrapped my arms around her waist, my fingers dancing against her belly bump. "Every part of you is mine, Aurora," I whispered into her ear. "And, Goddess, I love you more than anything."

Once Aurora finally crawled off me, she buried her face in my arms and kissed my shoulder, her thighs pressed together and small little whimpers escaping her lips. I glanced down at her and gently tucked some hair behind her ear, admiring the way the moonflowers' light reflected off her face.

After a couple of moments, I intertwined my fingers with Aurora's. "We need to talk about the stone. Before your surgery and during the Luna Ceremony after-party, my dad told me that only one person has wielded a stone like yours."

Aurora rolled onto her stomach and stared down at me, the flowers shimmering off her big eyes. She set her hand over my chest, right across the glowing scarlet scar, and furrowed her brows. "Who?"

"The Moon Goddess," I said.

"Selene?" she asked.

"Selene?" I asked. "Since when do you ever call her Selene?"

"I don't know …" Aurora said, eyes even wider and confusion written all over her face. "I don't know where that came from." She glanced up at the sky and spotted the faintest crescent moon among the stars. "What does this mean for me?"

According to Dad, the last person to use a stone like this was the Moon Goddess. And if she hadn't died like the rest of the previous users of the Malavite Stone had, did that make Aurora just like her?

"You have healing powers and super strength. Normal wolves don't just magically get powers from a stone, and you heard Medusa … not everyone can wield a stone like you can," I said, swallowing hard. "You have to be special. You have to be godlike."

CHAPTER 10

AURORA

"*G*odlike," I whispered on our way toward the Pink Moon Tavern, spotting the glowing neon sign through the thick brush.

There was surely no way I could be an immortal goddess. Godlike and being a god were two very different things.

Besides, my heart had stopped beating multiple times during the stone procedure, and on both occasions, I had come back to life. If I were immortal, I'd never die. That was how it worked, right? But if a heart stopped beating and the person lived on, what did that mean? How *had* I returned to life both times? Magic? A Moon Goddess curse?

I could be a zombie hound since I had hound blood, or I could be something *else* ...

And then again, in Helios's letter, he had said that Dawn had died by Nyx's hand.

Wrapping my arm around Ares's to ground myself, I continued down the path with him to a clearing in front of the tavern. Wolves hung around front, drinking milkshakes and chatting with each other about the war to come.

When I saw Marcel and Charolette sharing a milkshake through the large glass windows, I stopped and smiled. Ares looked back at me with furrowed brows, asking me with his eyes why I had suddenly paused. I nodded toward the windows and rested my head on his shoulder.

"They love each other," I whispered.

Inside the tavern, Charolette tore the paper wrapper off the edge of a straw, wrapped her lips around the end, and blew the other wrapper piece at Marcel's face. It hit him square in the nose, and he shriveled back, his silver hair falling into his face.

Charolette looked so happy and lively that it was hard to believe she was dying.

She tucked some hair behind his ear, smiled sweetly at him, and leaned in to kiss him softly on the mouth. Marcel tensed for the briefest moment and kissed her back, his lips still lingering on hers before he pulled away.

Butterflies fluttered in my stomach, a giddy feeling erupting through my body. I grasped Ares's hand tighter and pulled him into the Pink Moon Tavern, deciding to give them more privacy. They were just too damn cute not to watch. I loved them together, almost as much as I loved Ruffles and Pringle together.

"Aurora!" someone called to my right.

Elijah sat in a booth with two milkshakes in front of him, one full and the other nearly empty. I tugged Ares toward his table, sniffing the air and catching the scent of Adrian. They must've had a date here tonight too.

After quickly pulling the empty glass to his side of the table, he gestured for us to sit. "Just the couple I wanted to talk to tonight. I didn't have time to stay after the meeting this morning, but I, uh"—he scratched the back of his neck—"wanted to let you both know what's up."

Once we ordered milkshakes, we slid into the booth.

"What'd you want to talk to us about?" I asked.

"I'm not going to the underworld," he said, adjusting his thick glasses. "I think it's best for me to stay up here and continue to research the hounds, so I can give everyone some kind of advantage. If I find something, I'll make sure to relay the information to you. And if you are both going, I can oversee your pack while you're gone."

Ares tensed. "We won't be gone that long."

"We don't know how long it's going to take," I said, placing a hand on his thigh and hoping to calm him down. My stomach twisted into tight knots, the upbeat music playing through the tavern doing nothing to still my nerves. "It could be years."

The thought that our daughter might have to endure some terrible things in her lifetime finally sank in. We didn't know anything about the underworld yet—not the layout, not the terrain, not even if we would be able to survive for centuries.

"Alpha Ares! Your milkshakes," the woman shouted from the counter.

When Ares slid out of the booth to grab our shakes for us, I leaned across the table and stared at Elijah in fear. I hadn't quite said this out loud yet, but … with everything changing so quickly and his nightmares, I was afraid that things would just get worse for Ares. I desperately needed to figure out what had caused the red scar on his chest and if it had anything to do with Mars's disappearance.

After finding Helios's horseshoe in that field, I really believed Ares now and not Denise. Denise might've thought that this was separation anxiety, but … if my dreams were real, then his reality must be too.

"I'm afraid that he's losing it," I whispered.

Elijah looked over at Ares. "He seems fine to me. The same old cruel Ares."

"He says that Mars died during the hound attack, that his heart stopped beating and Mars left him. The doctor doesn't know what it is. She says it can't happen and that this is far more than her area of expertise. But ... he really did die."

A part of Ares had died.

How could someone go on with their life after something like *that* happened?

Elijah furrowed his brows in the same supportive manner he always did with me. "I would offer up another doctor, but none of mine have experience with DI—wait, you said he stopped breathing?" he asked. "And now, he's alive again, just like when our doctor put the stone in you?"

My eyes widened slightly, but then I shook my head. No, this was different, wasn't it? Ares didn't have the stone or any stone inside of him ... but he had that red scar. Did that mean something?

"He has a red scar right across his chest. It's glowing," I said.

Ares approached with two milkshakes and napkins between his teeth. I smiled up at my mate and grabbed the shakes from his hands. He sat down beside me, and I decided to change the subject for now. I didn't want Ares to feel bad.

"Ares thinks that the stone makes me godlike," I said.

"Your powers are as strong as a goddess's," Elijah said. "I've witnessed them with my own two eyes."

"She is a goddess," Ares said with so much confidence that it almost scared me.

"I'm not a goddess," I whispered, shaking my head and turning back to Elijah. While I was almost positive that I wasn't a goddess, that didn't mean that I didn't have something in my blood making me different.

It could be those damn hounds.

"Have you taken notice of two distinct types of hounds?" I asked.

Elijah raised his brows. "I ... I've seen some distinct differ-ences, but I never thought anything of it. It's a conversation I was having with one of my researchers earlier. She had dug into a book during the War of the Lycans about there being hellhounds and zombie-like hounds, like the ones we've fought. Hellhounds don't typically leave the underworld, but some of the stronger and more divine wolves can."

"Like Fenris?" I asked.

"Just like Fenris."

"Is there any way you can see if there is a difference between these hounds?"

"For me to see if they're different, I'd have to find both kinds to study their blood."

"What kind do you have now?"

"The kind like you," Elijah said. "Almost the same kind of blood, but who knows how your blood has changed since your body has accepted the stone? It might have created a transformation of some sort on your body."

"It's divine blood," Ares said, certainty lacing every word.

"How are you so sure of it?" I asked, brows furrowed as I looked over at my mate.

He had that stoic and divine look on his face again, and yet I could see a hundred images flash through his mind. And they weren't images of anything I had seen before when I was with him. They were images of the past, of him carrying me, of my vision I'd had earlier when my fingers brushed against his scar.

"Take a blood sample," I said to Elijah. "From both of us."

I needed to find out what all of this meant.

* * *

AFTER ELIJAH TOOK samples of our blood, he promised to get back to us about it as soon as possible. Ares and I returned to the pack house to turn in for the night, and yet even as I lay down in bed next to my mate, I couldn't help thinking about the possibility of having divine blood or of being a goddess.

It definitely couldn't be true, but Ares had seemed so sure, and with his glowing scar and the feeling of power swelling inside of me, something was definitely different. And we had to find out what his scar and my power meant before we left for the underworld.

Maybe it really did mean we were something magical. Or maybe my mind was just messing with me.

Moonlight flooded into the dark room, glinting off of Ares's sculpted face. He pulled me closer to him, his breath uneven against my bare skin. I breathed in his hazelnut scent and tried to relax in it, but thoughts rushed around too quickly through my mind for me to silence them.

All my life, I'd just wanted to be normal. I didn't want to be better or worse off than anyone. I'd wanted to be able to run with the wolves and be happy. Nothing more. But if it *was* true that I had divine blood, I could help so many people who were like me, who couldn't shift or couldn't protect themselves.

We lay there in silence for a good twenty minutes before Ares ground himself against my backside. He stuffed his face into the crook of my neck and growled so lowly that it almost sounded like a purr vibrating against my skin in the darkest of the night.

"A goddess," he whispered to me, drawing his nose up the side of my neck and letting his lips linger just above the top part of his mark. He flicked his tongue against it, making me whimper. "I knew it from the moment I saw you, Kitten."

My breath caught in my throat, my body tensing as he teased my pussy with his hardness. He rubbed himself on me, growing harder by the second and keeping his thrusts against me surprisingly calm and even.

"I'm not a goddess, Ares," I said, though I didn't quite believe the words myself.

I clenched and let out a breathy moan, all my worries disappearing for a few moments. He had always been good at getting me to relax, at helping me forget.

He growled—harsher and more guttural this time—and then

wrapped a hand around the front of my neck and pushed me onto my stomach. Straddling my backside, he ground his hips into mine from behind, rubbing his bare cock against my round ass. He gently pushed some hair behind my ear. "Stop lying to yourself," he said, tugging my throat up just enough and forcing me to look into the mirror beside our bed.

Ares was on top of me, the moonlight illuminating every one of his bulging muscles and making him look as if he were glowing. I sucked in a breath as he kissed, sucked, gnawed on his mark.

To anyone else, he might look like a savage monster about to ravage his prey.

But to me, he was the god of war who had a soft spot for me.

With his eyes glowing gold and his lips lingering on my neck, he grazed his canines against the mark he had left on my neck. "Watch as I *love* you tonight, Kitten."

Love me.

There weren't many times that Ares *made love* to me.

I stared at him through the mirror, watching as he spit on his hand, rubbed it against his cock, and thrust himself into me, pushing himself as deep as he could get. His scar glinted red again, the color lighting up the room and bringing back memories of him.

The pressure built up inside me, nearly tipping me over the edge.

"I said to watch," he growled into my ear, staring at me through the mirror's reflection.

I reopened my eyes and watched them smolder in the mirror, not my usual golden wolf color but a mixture of reds, oranges, and pinks.

My breath caught in my throat as they radiated more intensely, the closer I came to my orgasm. Ares stared at them in the mirror.

"Look at you," he mumbled against my skin, his slight stubble brushing against my neck and making me tingle. He grasped my chin lightly in his hand and pushed himself deeper. "Those eyes, Kitten," he said, quickening his thrusts. "They started glowing after the stone was put inside of you. Those eyes of yours aren't wolf or human eyes anymore."

Pressure rose in my core with every thrust. Ares kissed my neck and then gently shifted my chin, so I was kissing him. He slipped his tongue into my mouth, his lips devouring mine, like if they didn't, I'd disappear.

"They're divine," he murmured against my lips.

My fingers dug into the pillow, and my toes curled as pleasure pumped through me. Something about us, about this, about him made me feel so good and so powerful. Ares might think that the stone made me a goddess, but I had thought he was a deity of war since the moment I'd met him.

If I was truly divine, so was he.

"I love you, Kitten," he said against my ear, pushing himself into me one last time and stilling until he came.

I cried out into the night, feeling closer to him than I ever had before.

He pulled out slowly, wrapped his arms around my waist, and rolled back to his side, pulling me tightly into his arms. "I love you more than you will ever know, and I would do anything for you. You're my only strength."

Tears welled up in my eyes—beautiful, sweet tears. Though Ares loved me, he had always been so harsh, so uninviting, so terribly blunt. Hearing these words spoken so softly and truthfully and lovingly toward me … made my heart swell.

I cherished this man more than I cherished anyone.

And Mars might be gone for good, but Ares would forever be mine.

Nobody would step in the way.

Not even the gods of the underworld.

CHAPTER 11

ARES

*W*ith a thick layer of sweat covering my bare chest, I stood before my pack warriors, hands on my hips, and listened to Marcel's daily spiel about becoming stronger to protect this pack. He had been the pack trainer for years now, but only recently had the warriors in this pack started really stepping up their game.

Over the past couple weeks, everyone had seemed to be training more resiliently.

We always had, but now, we finally understood the danger we faced.

"Five-mile run," Marcel said, nodding to the woods around my pack. "Don't slow down. Don't stop. Keep running like your life depends on it because it fucking does. If we want to kill these fuckers and protect our families, we need to be fast, mentally and physically."

After the warriors shifted into their wolves midair and sprinted through the forest, Marcel glanced at Charolette with his lips pressed in a tight line. She stood off to the side, shifting from foot to foot and gnawing on the inside of her cheek.

She hadn't been able to run five miles in weeks now.

This week, her energy had seemed sapped, even from the smallest of tasks. And the thought of losing my sister tore me up on the inside. First Mom, then Mars ... I couldn't fucking lose her too. Besides Dad, she was the only family I had left.

"One mile," Marcel said to her, leaving no room for argument.

After nodding her head—her eyes much duller than they usually were—she pulled off her wig and her clothes and then shifted into a thinning, sickly wolf. Her usually thick fur had been growing thinner and thinner by the day, and there were patches that looked to have fallen out so much that I could see the thin white skin underneath.

I tore my gaze away from her and clenched my jaw.

Dwindling away.

She was fucking fading.

Aurora lingered by my side and glanced at Charolette. "Do you think I should—"

"You need to be strong, Aurora," Marcel said, tension in his voice. I couldn't tell if it was his usual anger or an incredible amount of hurt because of his mate. "Charolette will do what she can, but you need to hone your wolf's powers." He gestured to the forest. "Run."

With a frown, Aurora easily shifted into her wolf and glanced over at me, nodding to the forest. *"We need to find another way to contact Medusa,"* Aurora said through the mind link as we ran farther into the woods, the wind whipping through her brown fur. *"Her journal didn't leave a good taste in my mouth ... I feel like the hounds are going to come back soon."*

I growled at the thought of being attacked by another pack of hounds, my canines aching to rip into their flesh. Our luck, they'd attack when Aurora was giving birth to our pup. She'd be stressed out the entire time about both protecting our girl and hoping that I was staying safe while I slaughtered as many as I could outside.

And if Hella returned to our world without Helios—whoever that man was—we'd be in a shitload of trouble. While I was almost certain Aurora was a goddess, if she was giving birth, I couldn't let her focus on the hounds at all. They'd be my burden, and the last time I'd fought them, I'd lost Mars.

When we approached the five-mile mark, we walked back to the training field to start sparring. I tugged on some shorts and gazed into the forest, through the trees, to see Charolette and Marcel not having even moved a mile from their original starting position.

Palms posted on the ground and heaving over, Charolette shifted mid-run to catch her breath, shook her head, and slammed her fist into the ground, so hard that her knuckles bled and didn't heal. "I hate this," she whispered.

Pain shot through my body. I stared at her from across the forest and felt so incredibly hopeless, like my world was caving in on me. Charolette's ribs jutted out of her already-petite frame. More bruises lined her legs and arms. Dark circles lay under those bright eyes of hers.

My sister couldn't even make it through a mile run anymore.

This past week, Marcel had lowered her from a five-mile run to a mile run in hopes of keeping her wolf and her happy and healthy. She'd always loved running when she was a kid, and now, she couldn't even run half a mile without gasping for air.

"Ares," Aurora said, placing one hand on my bicep and glancing over at my sister. "Ares, what's wrong?"

The warriors, who were gathered in the center of the training field, started sparring with each other, throwing, biting, clawing to become stronger and faster and better fighters. But all I could do was stand there and look at my sister.

Charolette walked out from the woods and sat at the edge of the field, pulling on some clothes. She downed a bottle of water and watched the warriors with so much shame, shaking her head and allowing the tears to pour down her cheeks.

"My sister is dwindling away, Aurora," I said.

A couple of warriors glanced in our direction, and Aurora grabbed my hand, tugging me into the woods, where nobody could hear us.

"Ares," she whispered, grasping my face. "Not where she can hear you. I'm sure she knows it already."

My lips trembled, and I promised myself that I wouldn't cry.

I never cried.

Mars did. Not me.

"She's dying." I balled my hands into fists and hit the nearest tree with all my might, letting the tree crack and fall beside us, the thunderous bang echoing through the quiet woods. "She's fucking dying, and I can't do anything about it. I tried … I tried fucking hard to keep her alive."

Aurora glanced through the woods, toward the direction of our pack, and frowned. When she turned back to me, she had tears in her eyes—the same kind of tears that I wanted to shed but wouldn't allow myself.

"It's not your fault," Aurora said, rubbing my shoulder. "It has never been your fault."

I ripped myself away from her. "Yes, it is."

I couldn't protect her from death, just like I couldn't protect Mars from it or Mom from it or any of my damn packmates who'd died from the hound attacks from it. I was a fucking useless alpha if I couldn't do the one fucking thing I had been born to do—keep people safe.

"Calm down, Ares," Aurora said, reaching out for me and resting her hands on my chest.

When her fingers brushed against my glowing sanguine scar, all I could see was war. Moments flashed through my mind that I was sure I hadn't experienced before. I didn't know if it was the future or the past, but Aurora was with me, lying in my arms, her hands grasping my shoulders, her head buried into my taut chest.

AMID FIRE AND FLAMES, warriors were dying all around us. My body felt so weak, but I continued to push through people. Why was I bringing Aurora to safety? I didn't know. All I knew was that I wanted to be out in that war, killing the enemy, but I needed to make sure she wasn't in danger.

A pain shot through my chest, and a spear—my own spear, the same spear that could make any god fall to his knees in pain—ripped through my flesh, almost hitting Aurora. I stumbled to the ground, Aurora slipping from my arms.

I crawled to her, wanting to protect her with everything that I'd ever had, even though blood was gushing out of the wound and from my mouth, pouring down onto her stomach. Her gaze shifted from me to someone behind me, her eyes wide.

When I gazed back, my heart dropped. We were screwed.

"Run," I whispered to her. "Don't ever stop. Not even for me."

"LET ME TALK TO HER," Aurora said, pulling me out of the nightmares I was now having while awake. "Why don't you go train with Marcel? Blow off some steam. I'll chat with Charolette as soon as I can."

I pressed my lips together, holding all the hurt and pain inside of me.

I refused to let Aurora see her strong, warmonger alpha break down in tears. Again.

Aurora paused, intertwined our fingers, and kissed me right on the lips. "Are you going to be okay?" she mumbled. When I nodded, she pushed away some sweat-covered hair sticking against my forehead and said, "I need to hear it from you. Tell me that you're going to be okay."

She was pregnant with our daughter, the daughter who would see right through the fatherly facade I put up, the daughter we'd tell stories about Mars and wonder where he was, the daughter who'd stare up at me with Aurora's big eyes and ask if I was strong enough to protect her too.

And I didn't want Aurora to stress even more about my nightmares, about me worrying about Charolette, or even about me. I needed to be strong for her. I needed to grasp control of something in my shitty life.

"I'll be okay," I lied.

CHAPTER 12

AURORA

While Ares ran off to train with his pack, I stood at the edge of the forest and frowned, hurt rushing through every one of my veins. He had lied to me about being okay. It had been written all over his face and woven into every one of his words.

My heart ached for him. I wanted to see my mate happy again.

Mars might be gone, but that didn't mean I loved or thought any less of Ares. Whether he was Ares or Mars, he was still my mate, and I would do whatever I could to protect him even if it was from the monster inside of him.

Dragging my feet toward the pack, I shifted my gaze to Charolette. After exchanging a few harsh words with Marcel and poking a finger against his chest, she disappeared through the forest to walk back toward the pack house.

Quickly, I tugged on my shirt over my sports bra and hurried after her. Maybe if I learned how to control this power, I might be able to help heal her. I needed to try something because if she died, then Ares ...

I feared Ares would disappear from this world too.

But before I could run past Marcel, he snatched up my upper arm and yanked me back harshly. "Where do you think you're going?" he asked me, silver hair blowing in the strong Sanguine Wilds wind. "You need to be strong, Aurora. I don't know how many times I've had to tell you that this week."

"I need to talk to Charolette," I pleaded.

Marcel pursed his lips. "You haven't been able to train your wolf without problems for years, decades even. If you don't train, you will die down in the underworld." He clenched his jaw. "You saw how terrible those fucking hounds were. There will be more of them down in the underworld, and without you ..." He paused. "Without you, we'll all die."

Sucking on the inside of my cheek, I crossed my arms. Having the entire Malavite Stone inside of me not only gave me confidence to move freely and fight harshly, but I also had powers that nobody else knew about, except maybe Helios and those other gods.

Marcel was right. No matter how much I didn't want to admit it.

"Give me forty-five minutes of training, and then you can leave early to talk to her."

After glaring at him for a couple moments, I finally succumbed and nodded. I loved Charolette, but if we didn't train, then *everyone* might die. It was a tough decision, but I had a pup to think about too. I needed to be able to protect my baby girl.

So, I trudged back to the training field, found someone to fight, and gave it all I had for forty-five gruesome minutes until sweat dripped down my body and my chest heaved up and down. I even felt my baby kick a couple times, as if she were training with me too.

When I felt her, I smiled. She was going to be a fighter through and through.

* * *

BY THE TIME I finished training, the only thing I could think about was healing Charolette. Throughout practice, I had gone through scenario after scenario of ways to jump-start my powers because since that hound attack, I hadn't even figured out how to use them.

I wiped a towel down my chest and headed directly for the pack house, knowing that I'd find Charolette there. She didn't go out anymore by herself, like she used to, especially now that we were in a different pack.

Sitting in the grand living room that Mom had decorated with War of the Lycan artwork and canines she had gathered from over the years, Charolette was slumped over on the couch with tears running down her cheeks. When she saw me, she tried to push them away, but they just kept coming.

"Aurora," she whispered. "Why're you back so soon?"

Instead of giving her some bullshit excuse, I walked over to her, wrapped her in my arms, and held her to my chest. She was tense at first, but then she pulled me to her as tightly as she could and started heaving back and forth, hiccups escaping her lips and fingers digging into my shoulders.

"I'm sorry ... I'm so sorry ..." she kept mumbling, shaking her head and sniffling. "I'm so weak. I will never be able to protect this pack anymore. I'll hold you all back. I'll ... I'll be a burden to you all."

"Charolette, you're not a burden. You have shown an incredible amount of strength throughout your cancer and during your treatments." I wiped away a couple tears from her cheeks with my thumbs. "Don't think that you're going to hold us back when you're the one person holding us all together."

"But I can't even run anymore. I love running. My wolf loves running. We don't even have the energy to get through a mile." More tears streamed down her face. "I'm dying! I'm freaking dying, and I can't do anything about it!"

Tears welled up in my eyes, and I promised myself that I wouldn't cry. I had to be strong for her and for Ares. This must've been the hardest thing for her ... knowing that she's dying and not being able to fix it, feeling herself dwindle away and become weaker by the day.

I had to heal her. I had to try something.

But how? How could I heal someone when I had no freaking idea how to use my power in the first place? Did I try it and hope for the best? Think about using these powers that I knew nothing about? Did I have to be high on adrenaline to heal someone?

"Can you try to heal me?" she asked suddenly. "I heard a rumor that you healed Elijah."

While I didn't know how I had done it, I'd guess that it was sort of ... a natural instinct, something that had just happened when I was with him. I wasn't aware of why it'd happened. And I didn't know if I'd be able to heal her like I'd healed Elijah. His wound had been external, a wound I could physically see and heal.

Could I heal cancer?

"You're my last hope, Aurora," Charolette whispered, grasping my hand in her weak hold. Her hands felt so fragile and so thin that I could almost feel all the bones inside of it, poking into my palm.

"I'll do it, but I don't know if it'll work. I don't know how I even did it," I whispered.

I didn't want to get her hopes up for nothing. These new powers were so foreign to me.

"I need this, Aurora," she said, resting her forehead on mine. "I don't want to live like this anymore. I can't run. I can't enjoy my life anymore. My wolf is getting weaker by the moment. I need this more than anything. And if this doesn't work, I'm getting off my treatment and starting hospice."

CHAPTER 13

ARES

*M*arcel slammed my body against the ground, giving it his fucking all and driving me into the dirt. Sweat soaked his silver hair, clumping it together. A thunderous growl escaped his mouth. Rage burned within his dark eyes.

He hadn't said a word to me since Charolette had left.

Neither had I.

When he shuffled off me, he tied the locks back with an elastic and hummed angrily to himself. "Practice is over. We'll meet back here early tomorrow for another training session, focused on skill and technique. Don't be late."

I pushed myself off the ground and lingered back to talk to him.

Don't get me wrong; I hated fucking talking about my feelings. But today, Marcel looked like he needed it—or at least a long drink at the Pink Moon Tavern. I wiped away the sweat coating my body with my shirt and tossed my hoodie over my shoulder.

"You want to get a drink?" I asked.

Because, fuck, I needed one too.

Marcel cut his gaze to me, rolled his eyes, and nodded, following after me through the forest and toward Pink Moon Tavern. Though it was late afternoon, the sun was already setting upon the Sanguine Wilds, creating a sea of pinks, purples, and blues on the horizon.

We didn't say a word to each other until the neon lights glimmered in the distance. Wolves of all ages swaggered out of the front door with drinks and milkshakes, and some young kids played catch in the clearing, the ball nearly hitting the windows.

"I need this," Marcel said, snapping open the door and finding a seat at the bar to sit in. "So fucking badly."

Sliding onto a stool beside him, I nodded. "Me too."

The bartender walked over to us. "The usual?"

"Mmhmm," Marcel and I responded at the same time.

"Is it fucking bad that they know our order?" he asked.

My lips curled into the best smile I could muster. "No."

After the waitress placed two glasses of rum in front of us, Marcel shot his back almost instantly. "I'm a fucking mess. I don't know what to do with Charolette. She didn't want me to be part of her life for so fucking long, and now that I am … it hurts, seeing her like this. Dwindling away into nothingness."

I pressed my lips together and took a sip, the drink going down smoothly. "I know."

It wasn't the same, but I understood what he was going through. Charolette didn't let many people into her life, and even being close to her all these years … I couldn't fucking take seeing her like this anymore.

For months, years even, I'd tried to find that stone for her.

Now, that was hopeless. She hadn't even wanted the damn thing.

"It's fucking hard." Marcel stared emptily at the counter. "Whenever I sleep beside her, her body feels more and more fragile every night. I'm afraid that one night, I'm going to accidentally roll over while sleeping and snap her bony body in half."

He balled his hands into fists and thrust them down through the air, stopping millimeters away from the counter before he broke it. When he unraveled his fists, blood pooled out of his palms from his claw marks.

"I don't know how much longer she has," Marcel said, voice breaking. "And I hate it."

My chest tightened at his words, and I drew my finger around the rim of my cup. "It's hard, loving a sick person, but it's harder, being one."

In my lifetime, I had been on both sides of that broken coin. Loving Aurora without bounds, even when she couldn't shift and I thought I would tear her apart, was the easiest damn thing I had ever done. Like Charolette meant everything to Marcel, Aurora was my world.

But being sick in the fucking head was an uphill battle every fucking day of my life.

Nothing compared to the hurt, anguish, and torment that I felt.

Not only for myself, but also for the burden I put on so many other people.

"All we can do for the people we love is be there for them," I said, staring off into space. "Be there for them and support them through all the challenges the Moon Goddess throws at us. We must be prepared for the worst but hope for a better tomorrow."

CHAPTER 14

AURORA

"*P*lease, be still, Charolette," I whispered, kneeling down in front of her.

While I wanted to heal her nearly more than I had wanted to be able to shift easily again, healing her sickness wouldn't solve all her problems. Hell, was this even possible? It was cancer —*fucking cancer*.

Cancer wasn't an open wound that could be bandaged.

And she'd already tried so many treatments that didn't work.

Charolette stared down at me with big, glossy eyes and shuffled upright on the suede couch. I placed my hands on her knees and closed my eyes, begging myself—that inner goddess or whatever I had inside of me—to heal one of my best friends.

But leukemia was in the blood, and blood was throughout the entire body, not just in one concentrated spot, like Elijah's fatal wound had been. It was nearly impossible to heal the blood in every vessel of her body.

Impossible, but I had to try.

I squeezed my eyes closed.

Focus, Aurora. Heal Charolette. Think blood. Think about Ares, how happy he'll be after learning that she can live her life in happiness and peace without the constant fear of a cruel, early ending to her life.

Four minutes passed and then five. I gripped Charolette's knees so tightly that I was afraid I'd leave dark bruises on her sensitive skin. Pressing my lips together, I desperately beckoned the same power that had run through my body during the hound attack.

Yet nothing.

This wasn't working.

I needed something immense to get my power flowing, something to bring my inner goddess out. And as if the Moon Goddess had heard me, the window behind Charolette shattered into thousands of small shards.

Two hounds burst through the front window, their canines dripping with saliva, their sharp claws extended nearly three inches from their paws, and their eyes blacker than the darkest night.

Screaming, Charolette leaped up and away from the beasts. I pushed her and Ruffles behind me, not wanting either of them to die by these filthy monsters' canines, and then shifted into my wolf form. Adrenaline pumped through my body, and I latched my teeth into one hound's neck, killing him instantly.

Throat snapping, he fell to the ground at my feet. With sanguine foam oozing from his mouth, the second hound stalked closer to Ruffles, who stood in front of Charolette. Ruffles lowered her head and growled, her body small in front of the colossal hound.

With a swipe of his paw, he threw her against the wall but not before she caught him in the eye with her tiny claws. She hit the wall with a hard thud, headfirst, and I jumped into the air to catch her body between my teeth before she fell onto the ground.

After gently placing her down, I snatched the hound's tail as he approached Charolette, swung him around twice, and released his body to let him smack right through our living room wall, where he had thrown my Ruffles.

The wall broke into pieces, his body flying through the air and into the other room. Before he had the chance to recover, I sprinted through the hole in the wall and sank my canines into his left leg, ripping it off.

Wanting him to hurt, I tore each of his pathetic limbs from his body and clawed my way through every one of his guts until my paws were drenched in blood and none of his organs were even recognizable anymore.

Even Ruffles came over and batted at his face with her paws until he bled.

When I was certain both hounds were dead, I transformed into my human form and hurried into the living room to check on Charolette, who had taken the brunt of the attack of the monsters flying through the window.

She stood at the kitchen door with wide eyes, grasping the huge gash in her thigh. Shards of glass were suspended in her flesh, and the wounds weren't healing one single bit. Her sick body wouldn't allow her wolf to use her powers.

Adrenaline blasted through me, just like it had when I healed Elijah.

This might work. It just might freaking work.

"Move your hands, Charolette," I said. "Quickly."

Kneeling in front of her, I placed my hands over her wound and closed my eyes. The gash started to seal together underneath my trembling and bloodied hands. And once it closed entirely, I continued to pump my power into her, hoping to the gods that this worked because I needed her to stay alive.

She didn't deserve to die from cancer.

Nobody did.

The longer I held my hands against her flesh, the faster my energy depleted. After another five minutes, I let go and nearly doubled over, my entire body beyond drained of energy, adrenaline, and vigor.

While her open wounds healed, the bruises on her thighs and on her arms didn't.

Again. I had to try again.

I placed my hands on her body again and squeezed my eyes shut.

Heal, Aurora. Heal.

Another five minutes. Still nothing.

"Come on," I said out loud. "Please! Please. This has to work."

Ruffles nudged her head against my thigh, as if to push me away. My chest heaved up and down, my breaths becoming short and uneven. I couldn't just stop now. I needed to save her. I needed to give her whatever I had left.

If I couldn't save her, Mom would be right—with or without the Malavite Stone, I was the weakest wolf that had ever graced the Sanguine Wilds. I didn't deserve to hold such power inside my body. I didn't deserve the stone.

"You cannot and will not be able to heal her," someone said behind me.

"I have to," I said, trying harder.

Someone placed their hands on my shoulders and gently pulled me away. "You can't."

My eyes widened slightly, recognizing the voice and the touch. I twisted my head to see Medusa standing over us, thick strands of hair slithering around under her seafoam-green veil, which shielded her eyes.

"Medusa," I whispered in disbelief that she stood in my house.

Hopefully, she had received the note that we'd left her and was here to talk. I needed to ask her so much about the underworld and how to get down there. Now that the hounds were back, we needed as much information as possible.

Charolette stared up at her with wide eyes. "Who are you?" she asked, voice soft.

Turning my attention back to her, I grasped Charolette tighter. "I healed my friend before," I said to Medusa. "I need to try to heal Charolette too. She's dying, and she deserves to live more than anyone that I know."

Medusa rested a hand on Charolette's shoulder, paused, and grimaced. "Just as I thought," she said. "I know you've healed someone before, Aurora, but you won't be able to heal her. Her death has been sealed by Hella."

Hella.

Claws ripped out of my fingers. Hella was doing this because she hated me. She'd made Charolette worse because of some divine war that I had taken absolutely no part in. Why'd she have to take this out on her? Why couldn't it have been me?

Give me the cancer. Give me the death. Hurt me. Not my friends.

"My dear, Hella doesn't know that this young woman is your family. If Hella knew, she'd be dead already," Medusa continued. "But she's already marked her for death, and she is not a goddess who goes easy on her victims. Once her claws sink in, she doesn't take them out."

"Is there any way to heal her, any way to stop this?" I asked, desperate for something.

After glancing between Charolette and me, Medusa grabbed my arm and pulled me into the other room, lowering her voice so only I could hear her. She pulled the veil back, so I could see her piercing green eyes.

"There is nothing *you* can do, but it's rumored that some people can make deals to spare their loved ones' lives in exchange for their own. Someone came to her a long time ago to give his life to spend in the underworld for the person he loved to be healthy for a few more years. Hella accepted his request. But she would never accept this deal from you. She already wants you dead in her own evil ways."

"But from someone else?" I asked.

Anything. Anyone. I needed hope.

"*Possibly*," Medusa said.

"How?" I asked.

"That's too much for today. I must go. I don't have much time."

"It's okay." I threw my arms around her and pulled her closer to me. "Thank you so much for this. Thank you for giving us hope."

It wasn't certain, but it was hope that Charolette might live … as long as someone sacrificed their life for her.

Taken aback, Medusa tensed in my embrace. Then, she finally relaxed and patted my back, her fingers moving gently against my hair, and the wolf-like snakes on her hair slithered out from underneath her veil, wrapping around me.

When she finally pulled away, tears filled her eyes for some reason. "I must go."

"Did you get my note?" I asked.

"Yes, but I must go now. I have more pressing matters with the underworld." She thrust a slip of paper into my hand that had a single word written on it: cave. "For now, I wanted to tell you to meet me here tomorrow. That's the best I can offer you. A war is coming."

I glanced at the dead hounds. "The war is here."

Medusa pulled her hand away from mine and re-veiled herself. "You must be prepared. Hella is the goddess of death, and she wants to slaughter anyone and everything you love."

CHAPTER 15

AURORA

*W*ith my arms wrapped around my knees, I rocked back and forth on the patio chair and thought about everything that had happened in the past hour. After I'd told Charolette that I couldn't fix her, she'd cried her eyes out in her bedroom so loudly that I could hear it from here.

It hurt me almost as much as it was hurting her. But I could do nothing to help. Just by trying to heal her, all my energy was zapped from my body. This was her last chance, and I wasn't strong enough to rip her from Hella's grasp.

Unless I found someone who would trade their life for hers, her fate was sealed.

And I knew Marcel would trade his life in an instant, but I feared asking him, because if we lost him, we might lose the war.

From afar, Marcel and Ares walked up the path toward the pack house, chatting quietly with each other about something that they must not have wanted me to hear because when they reached me, they stopped completely.

"What's wrong with you?" Marcel asked.

When Charolette's cries echoed through the house and spilled onto the porch, Marcel ripped open the front door, fear all over his face. "What happened to her? Why is she crying? Did you hurt her?"

"No, I just ..." I stared down at the wooden porch and frowned. "I couldn't heal her."

Marcel's face fell. "She asked you?"

"Yes," I whispered, tears welling up in my eyes. "And I couldn't. But I ... I might know something that could. Go comfort her, and we can talk about it later. Nothing is certain though, Marcel, so please don't tell her or get your hopes up."

After a moment, Marcel nodded curtly and said, "I won't," before disappearing into the house.

When he left, I closed my eyes and sighed. Hiding secrets fucking sucked, but I didn't want Charolette to know because she'd be against this idea. And if Charolette talked to Fenris, her biological father, again because she wanted to get to know him and even mentioned that Marcel traded his life for her, then she might really die.

Ares knelt in front of me and placed a moonflower on my lap, giving me a crooked half-smile that didn't reach his eyes. "I got this for you," he whispered, gnawing on the inside of his lip. He almost looked nervous as he rubbed his big hands up and down my thighs.

"I don't deserve it," I said, refusing to touch the flower. "I couldn't heal your sister."

"You tried," Ares said, wrapping my hand around the stem. "That's what counts."

I stared into the house through the shattered window. Marcel walked into the living room with Charolette, who was smiling again even if that spark didn't twinkle in her eyes like it usually did. She giggled, the sound drifting out into the night and making me warm.

Charolette was happy again, and I'd tried.

That was all that mattered.

I just wished she had gotten her happy ending.

"Why is the window shattered?" Ares suddenly said, pushing back his taut shoulders and examining the scene in the living room through the window. "There's glass everywhere and blood on the carpet."

"Two hounds came out of nowhere and attacked us."

"Hounds?" Ares asked, nostrils flaring.

"Yes, hounds." I twirled the moonflower between my fingers and watched the moonlight bounce off the petals, remembering my dream where I'd fastened a crown of moonflowers on Nyx's head, her indigo hair glistening with streaks of white because of these flowers.

It had been a beautiful sight yet a haunting memory.

"Why are you so distanced from this, Aurora?" Ares snapped.

"It's fine," I said, unable to feel anything other than sorrow. "I killed them. But if they're just appearing out of nowhere now, we have bigger problems than them just attacking us. We have to be ready at all times. They're coming."

Though Ares growled, he didn't say anything else, just paced back and forth on the porch with his hands running through his thick brown hair and an unreadable expression on his sculpted face.

"You guys want to have pretzels with us?" Marcel shouted at us from the kitchen.

"Come on," Ares said, tugging me to my feet.

I shrugged him off me, still feeling so … so … detached from everything. I wanted to be alone to figure this shit out. I didn't like the feeling of hopelessness and uselessness. Mom's opinions were still heavy on my mind.

"I'll be inside in a bit," I said.

Ares stared at me for a couple moments, his anger fading to sadness, and then he stepped into the house, shutting the door a bit harder than I'd expected. I closed my eyes and sank deeper into the rocking chair.

Feeling like this sucked, I wondered if this was how Ares had been feeling since Mars had died.

"Hey," someone called.

When I reopened my eyes, Elijah was walking down the pathway to the pack house with Adrian, zipping up his jacket as the wind blew leaves across the stone walkway. I extended my legs off the chair and sat up taller again.

"Elijah, what are you doing here?" I asked.

Ares sauntered back out of the house with a plate of soft pretzels and *without* the usual hot cheese, like Mars always brought out. I gave him my best smile when he offered me some and grabbed one from the plate.

"I have some news regarding your blood." Elijah walked up the porch steps and leaned against the wooden pole beside Adrian. Then, he took a deep breath and scratched the back of his head. "I didn't have any samples to go off of from divine gods and goddesses though."

I leaned forward. "What did you find?"

"Your blood has changed," Elijah said to me. "It still has an element of hounds, but there is something in it ... something that started to glow when I tested it." He shook his head, as if he couldn't believe it himself. "And, Ares"—he looked over at Ares— "your blood is nearly identical to Aurora's, except without the hound mixture."

"What does that mean?" I whispered.

"Like I said, I don't know if it's divine blood because I don't have anyone to test it against, but it is different. The healing properties are tremendously strong. The blood regenerates at extreme speeds. If I had to make a prediction, I'd say that it has aspects of divinity in it, and that you both are descendants of gods and goddesses."

CHAPTER 16

ARES

*G*ods and goddesses. Not able to heal Charolette. The hounds. War.

We spent the next hour talking to Elijah about it, but I still couldn't wrap my head around *all* of this. There was too much going on for all of us to handle alone anymore, and sometime during the chat, I realized that I missed seeing my mate smile often.

All we did was stress lately.

And I wanted to change that tonight. I wanted to help her relax. To give her an unforgettable night.

After talking to Elijah, we walked back into the pack house to find Charolette curled up in Marcel's arms in the living room while watching a movie. She looped a piece of his silver hair around her finger, tugging on it slightly and staring up at him instead of the TV.

Aurora bounced on her toes beside me, creepily watching them from the kitchen and grinning at me. "How cute are they?!"

she whisper-yelled at me, placing a hand to her mouth and giggling behind it. "Oh goodness, I have butterflies."

I playfully rolled my eyes at her. "I can be cute too."

"And how's that?" Aurora asked, one hand on her hip and her lips curled into an evil smile.

"How's that?" I asked, stalking closer to her, forcing her to walk backward into the kitchen and then trapping her between me and the kitchen counter. "I'll show you how that is." I wrapped my arms tightly around her waist to pull her closer to me, and when she was flush against my chest, I dug my fingers into her sides to tickle her.

She giggled and squirmed in my grasp. "Oh Goddess, Ares!" She slunk down to the ground, maneuvering her way out of my hold until she doubled over in front of me and grasped her sides. "You know how much I hate being tickled."

"You don't hate it, Kitten," I said.

She loved it. Secretly.

Once she stood, she pointed to the door. "I'm making pretzels again. Mama is hungry. Go get the bedroom ready. We can"—she wiggled her brows—"have another tickle party later, if you know what I mean."

Amused, I walked toward the door and glanced back at Aurora's sexy, pregnant ass. She had a goofy smile on her face and couldn't stop laughing as she took the pretzels from the box and stuffed them into the microwave.

Ruffles meowed at me to go into the other room, telling me to follow Aurora's orders. I arched my brow at the gray ball of fur and walked down the hall, and then I collapsed on the bed in our room.

A couple moments later, Aurora walked into our bedroom with a plate of soft pretzels, the salt and bread rolling around on the plate. Ruffles followed her into the room, swaying her gray tail from side to side and shutting the door behind her.

"No cheese?" I asked, grabbing the plate and setting it on the unsteady bed.

Snatching it back, Aurora pulled out a folding serving tray she stored under the bed for times like these and set the plate on top of it. Then, she hopped onto the bed and stole a pretzel piece right from my hand.

"You like the cheese?" she asked, sticking the pretzel into my mouth. "I thought that was a Mars-only thing."

My lips curled into a fragile smile, a lingering warmth spreading throughout my chest. Earlier, when I'd brought out pretzels *without* the cheese to Aurora on the porch—by complete accident—she'd looked so sad.

Maybe she had always thought that both of us liked the cheese, but only Mars really had. I ate it sometimes for her because she loved it too. Never quite for me. Yet for her to make that distinction meant everything to me.

It was such a small, almost-laughable thing.

But Mars and I weren't the same person. Over the years, sometimes, people might have thought that we liked the same things, even our closest family. And to have Aurora recognize that this was mainly a Mars thing made me feel different.

"You could've still brought it for you," I said.

"Yeah, but"—she shrugged and plopped another into her mouth—"this is good too."

We continued to eat in silence. I brushed my toes against her every now and then, the feel of her skin against mine calming even the worst parts of my mind down for a bit tonight. After we finished, she set the serving tray to the side and glanced over at me.

"Are you still hungry?" she asked, lips curled into a smirk.

I arched my brow. "Why?"

"Because"—she spread her legs and placed her hand on her cunt through her soaked panties, instantly making me hard—"I'm horny, and I have something for you to eat. Your kitten's cunt is aching for you."

"Is that right?" I asked, drawing my tongue against my canines.

"My big, bad alpha must be hungry." She grasped her panties in her fist and pulled them right between her glistening pussy lips, her swollen clit stuffed between them. She ground her core against them, soaking them even further. "Come eat."

Gliding my tongue against my lips, I crawled between her legs and yanked her toward me. I dipped my head and grasped her underwear by my teeth, ripping them off by their seams. After stuffing them into her filthy mouth, I placed my hot mouth on her folds.

Tongue rolling over her clit, eyes gazing up at her, I thrust a finger into her pussy and ate her like the wild, savage alpha that I was. I groaned against her, dragging my tongue down her folds to her entrance. When I pulled my finger out of her, I sucked it into my mouth and licked off all her juices.

Kissing back up her body, I pulled up her shirt, sucked one of her nipples into my mouth, and tugged on it gently. Aurora arched her back, and I ground my hips into the mattress to relieve some of the pressure in my dick.

Aurora squirmed under me as I sucked harder on her breast.

"Beg, Aurora," I grunted against her, pressing my cock against her entrance and aching to thrust it right inside her. I dragged my teeth against the pink bud. "I love hearing your sweet little moans."

She grasped the sheets and tugged up on them, whimpering.

"Come on, Kitten," I taunted, pressing the head of my dick a bit harder against her drooling cunt. I tugged up on her nipple between my teeth and let it go, her breast bouncing back down. "You can beg, can't you?" I slipped a hand between her legs and rubbed her clit until she clenched. "Your pussy is *aching* for it."

"Please, Ares," she pleaded desperately.

Just as I was about to thrust it inside of her, I cocked a brow at her and shook my head at my mate. "You know better than that. Please what?"

"Please, Alpha."

I slowly pushed myself inside of her, letting her feel every inch of me. "Good girl, Kitten," I murmured into her ear, brushing some long brown hair out of her face. I moved my knees closer to her ass, lifting her hips off the bed slightly to get deeper inside of her.

"You're so"—I thrust hard and deep into her—"fucking"—another thrust—"good for me."

Instead of viciously pounding into her, I placed my lips on hers, kissing her softly. Our tongues moved together in a gentle rhythm as I gently thrust in and out of her.

"More," she mumbled to me. "Please, I want more."

I sucked her bottom lip between my teeth, thrusting faster into her and staring down at those big eyes that I had fallen madly in love with. "Fuck," I whispered, moving faster. "I fucking love you."

When she shuddered and relaxed into the mattress, I grunted at the sight of my mate's orgasm and spilled my load deep in her cunt. When I finished, she wrapped her arms around my shoulders and pulled me down to kiss me.

"I love you too, Ares. I will be with you through everything. You're never alone."

Collapsing by her side, I closed my eyes and breathed in her calming scent, finally relaxing for tonight.

* * *

"I TOLD everyone that I'd be with Nyx," Dawn whispered into my ear, her soft and plump lips moving up the column of my neck and lingering right below the angle of my jaw. "Nobody thinks I'm here with you."

"It's dangerous," I said, shaking my head, but I couldn't help drawing her closer.

Something about Dawn had always exhilarated me. When I was in the middle of battle, seeing the morning light flicker through the trees or feeling the dew under my feet instead of blood, it was tranquility—a feeling that I never thought I'd be able to explain.

I was war.

Yet she felt like my peace.

I wrapped my arms around her legs and pulled her on top of me, pushing her brown hair out of her face so I could see her refreshing smile. "It's dangerous to tell everyone that you're with Nyx while you're with me," I continued. "Hella wants to kill you for being with me, and Nyx's brother doesn't like outsiders."

"Hella has wanted to kill me for being with you for years, and she hasn't yet. She hasn't even tried. She's not strong enough to kill me, especially not when you're by my side. And, plus"—she drew a finger up the side of my neck, touching my scars—"gods can't die."

My lips curled into a smile, and I grasped her waist and rolled us over, burying my face into her neck. "I thought you hated me," I said, fingers digging into her sides to make her giggle. "What happened to you being terrified of me, Dawn?"

She let her fingers glide against my chest. "I've realized that the god of war has a soft side that not many people get to see." She smiled at me and pushed some hair away from my face, drawing her fingers down the scar that cut through my eyebrow. "I'm one of the lucky ones."

"You're the only one," I corrected.

Nobody else saw this side of me.

"The only one," she whispered, as if the words meant everything to her.

In the midst of a battle, I clutched a spear in my left hand and Aurora's hand in the other. With enemy blood smeared across my chest and an insatiable ache to kill, I pushed Aurora back. "Get behind me."

Yet she walked ahead of me with a pack of rogue wolves behind her, who were ready to pounce on our enemies from the underworld. Each rogue bared its long, bloodied canines, lowering their heads and analyzing the hounds.

"I'm not one of your men, Ares," Aurora said, eyes shifting between hundreds of dawn colors and shades—pinks and oranges and yellows. "I'm a goddess who will always fight beside you. You don't need to save me."

* * *

Someone slipped a silver sword right through her heart. She stared at me with wide eyes, blood dripping from her lips, gushing out of her mouth, pouring onto the ground. "Ares," she whispered, dropping to the dirt.

* * *

A hound ripped off her arm, throwing it across the forest.

They started to close in.

I couldn't find her.

She was gone.

Gone ...

I'd let her die.

* * *

The last thing I saw was her.

She wasn't there with me, but I saw her spirit, could feel her fingers glide over my shoulders and chest, could see her pretty little smile warm me.

Yet all I could feel was helplessness.

* * *

I STOOD in Medusa's ancient home, shaking my head back and forth. "She's not gone for good. She can't be. She's still alive. She always comes back to fucking life." My teeth were clenched.

I couldn't lose her for good. I fucking couldn't.

Aurora was the only fucking person who calmed me the fuck down.

She was the only fucking person who I loved.

"She's gone, Ares," Medusa said. "Her soul will live on, but her body is gone."

"It can't be. It fucking can't."

Aurora lay on Medusa's kitchen table with claw marks and bite marks all over her body. I brushed my fingers against all the fatal scars that should've killed her in the past two thousand years we'd been together, but hadn't. Why had this one been different? Why had she died now?

I should've been with her to protect her, but I hadn't been.

I hadn't been there.

I gripped one of Medusa's ceramic vases in my hand and threw it against the wall, watching it shatter. Rage rushed through me. I wanted to fucking kill all the people who'd had a hand in this. I would kill them. Nobody would get away with this.

"Ares, settle down," Medusa said. "Getting angry will only get you killed too."

I stormed out of the house. "She's the only woman I'll ever love."

I didn't care if avenging her would kill me.

She was mine, and I'd failed to protect what was mine yet again.

Mortals would pay. Wolves would pay. Gods would pay for her death.

CHAPTER 17

AURORA

*D*escendants of divines.
Is that what we are?

I gnawed on the inside of my cheek, stared up at the blank ceiling in our bedroom, and shook my head, a thin layer of sweat covering my lower back. Maybe that was what Elijah thought, but how could I *feel* those memories if I was just a descendant?

Ares tossed and turned in our bed, brows furrowed and a fearful expression on his sculpted face. I pulled the blankets over his naked body, hoping some kind of warmth and weight would calm him down.

Even Ruffles sat on his chest with her big baby belly, but it didn't calm him at all.

I didn't know if I should wake him up or let the nightmares continue. Ares didn't deserve to have these dreams every night, but if he didn't sleep, he'd be so tired during the day, and he wouldn't be at his best. I wanted to get more help for him soon. I needed to invite the therapist to come over again because trying to calm Ares down by myself wasn't working.

But neither was Denise, especially if Ares didn't want help.

After blowing out a breath, I decided to let him sleep. Ruffles crawled onto my chest and purred, licking my face with her coarse tongue, as if to say good night. Almost immediately, she fell into a deep cat sleep, as if Ares shifting around in the bed didn't bother her.

It bothered me, just not as badly as the storm outside.

Wind whipped tree branches against the window, creating grotesque shadows on the bed. Rain pounded against the roof so hard that it sounded like Helios's horses galloping through the night. Lightning struck through the night sky every couple moments, making Ruffles open one eye because it interrupted her beauty sleep.

"Charolette, please!" Marcel pleaded, his voice drifting through the thin walls. "Please, don't do this ..."

They had been arguing since Ares had fallen asleep. From the bits and pieces I'd heard of their conversation, it sounded like Charolette had just broken the worst news to Marcel, and Marcel wasn't taking it lightly.

Except, I had never heard Marcel this emotional.

He was usually pissed the fuck off, not voice-wavering sad.

"I can't," Charolette said. "I have to do this. Please, just accept my decision."

I rubbed my hand over my face and prayed to the Moon Goddess that I'd get some sleep tonight. I had so much on my mind, including my conversation with Elijah earlier and meeting Medusa tomorrow evening at the cave. I needed to have a clear head, so I wouldn't forget to ask her everything that I desired.

We were running out of damn time.

I stared up at the ceiling and rested my hand over my bump, feeling our baby kick. While werewolf pups usually took three months to come to full term, barely a month had passed, and I already felt huge. She was growing faster than typical werewolf pups did, which only confirmed what Elijah had told us earlier ... *divinity*.

Ares turned again, and I placed his hand on my stomach in his sleep. He relaxed slightly, his fingers curling into my bump. Our pup kicked against my stomach, hitting him right in the hand, and I swore he smiled.

My angry alpha freaking smiled at the feel of our pup.

Tears welled up in my eyes, and I bit my lip to hold in my whimpers. I wished Mars were here with us. I loved Ares, but I missed Mars so much in times like these. Mars had wanted pups, had dreamed of putting a pup inside of me and watching her grow.

If he only knew how strong our pup already was ...

He would have loved watching her grow in my tummy and kissing my stomach as she kicked.

My entire body tensed as I tried to hold myself from outright trembling next to Ares. All those late nights we'd spent talking with each other, when Mars used to feed me pretzels with that damn hot cheese, sweet little moments that I would never experience again.

It hadn't really hit me until now.

Mars was gone.

Really gone.

And he would never come back to me.

Tears slid down my cheeks, and I let them flow. I had been so occupied with the hounds, with protecting my pack and my pup that I hadn't found time to really think about how much I'd lost when he passed on from this world.

Not only had Ares lost half of himself, but I'd lost half of me too.

Mars was my mate, and I ... I had fucking lost him for good.

I closed my eyes and remembered when I had seen his ghost the other morning, running through the woods and to the lake where we had first met. For the slightest moment, I'd thought he was still alive, and I'd thought that we could spend the rest of our lives together again.

But death was a bitch.

"Forever yours, Kitten," he had said to me.

His last fucking words.

Balling the bedsheets in my fists, I ripped my claws right through them. Mars would want me to be strong. For Ares. For our pup. For our pack. So, I wouldn't give up now. I wouldn't give in to the pain. I had to make the hard decisions, so we could all live in peace someday.

Nothing would get in my way, not my doubt, not my sorrow, not myself.

And hopefully, when I met Medusa tomorrow at the cave, I would get as much information out of her as I could. I grabbed Ares's hand on my bump and intertwined our fingers. Ares might've been my rock for so long, but now, I needed to be strong for us.

CHAPTER 18

AURORA

"*L*et me out!" *I screamed, grasping on the thick divine chains bound to my neck.* "*Nyx!*"

Nyx walked down the stone palace steps to the dungeon filled with rotting corpses, rats, and an overwhelming stench of blood. Hella stood at the edge of my cell, one hand on her hip and her white eyes fixed on Nyx.

"*Will Nyx do it?*" *she asked Erebus, Nyx's brother.*

Erebus pushed Nyx toward my cell. "*If she wants me to let her roam free one day.*"

When Nyx reached my cell doors, my heart stopped beating. I sat in the cell with my energy quickly depleting and my eyes desperate to close. I didn't know how long I had been here. Days, weeks maybe.

All I knew was that I wouldn't stop struggling until I got to see Ares again.

"*Nyx! Let me out, please!*" *I shouted.* "*They're going to torture me down here.*"

She was my only hope, but I knew how this would end from Helios's letter.

Erebus pushed Nyx into the cell with me and shut the door behind her. "Tear her to pieces. I want your lover to hurt. I want him to hate you. I want him to try to come down here and kill you, so you can kill his ass because you're mine, Nyx."

"No, Nyx! Please, don't listen to him," I pleaded with her, tears streaming down my face. "You can't kill immortals. You can't ..." I whispered, but I knew differently. "Just let me go. Please, let me go."

Hella laughed right in my face. "Darling, you shouldn't have touched Ares, a man who wasn't yours. You are going to get everything you deserve." Hella turned to Nyx. "Make it hurt oh-so good."

"Ares has never been yours!" I screamed and then turned to Nyx. "You can try to kill me, Nyx ... but you won't be able to. No god has died—ever."

"Not true," Erebus said, lips curled into a smirk. "Nyx killed one just last year. She's the only goddess able to tear another divine to pieces. All those rumors those earthly gods have been whispering about are true. You should've believed them."

Nyx turned to me, her nails lengthening into talons.

"It's not true, Nyx," I begged. "I know you. You're not bad. You're good ..."

"It's true," Nyx said.

She stepped toward me and mouthed the words, This is for Helios. He won't leave earth because you live there. He's obsessed with you, and I want him for myself.

"Please, don't do this," I begged. "Please. I need to see Ares again."

I needed to see him. One last time.

Before I could react, she swiped her talons across my throat and killed me.

I SHOT up in the bed, gasping for air and clasping my hand over my neck. "Ares!"

Unlike my nightmare, blood wasn't pouring from my throat, yet I still held my hand tightly against the flesh, afraid that it would if I didn't. My heart thrashed against my rib cage, worries racing through my mind.

That was what had happened.

Hella had wanted to have Ares for herself, Nyx had wanted Helios for herself, and both of those men had wanted to be with me for some ungodly reason. I completely understood Ares's reasoning for wanting to spend eternity with me, but Helios?

How did he fit in?

"Ares!" I shouted again, slowly peeling my hand from my throat.

When the bedroom door slammed open, Ares bolted into the room from the connected bathroom with his eyes opened wide and his hair ruffled from tossing and turning all night in bed. He scooped me up into his strong arms and held me to his taut chest.

"What's wrong, Kitten?"

Tears streamed down my face, and I grasped him tightly. "You're here."

"Of course I'm here. What's wrong?"

"I just had a nightmare," I whispered, feeling so weak.

Ares had nightmares every night, but he didn't wake up with tears pouring down his face.

"About what?" he asked, sitting and leaning against the headboard.

"Dawn's death," I whispered. "It felt like I was her, and she was me. It felt so real ..."

Suddenly, another bedroom door slammed closed in the house. I jumped in Ares's arms, my heart pounding even harder, and scurried out of his arms, not wanting to detail my nightmare further and mention Helios.

"That sounded like Charolette," I said, tugging him to the kitchen and hoping he wouldn't pry. It was self-centered and hypocritical because I always wanted him to talk to me about what he was going through, but I just didn't want to make anything worse with him.

Strands of silver hair in his face, Marcel sat at the kitchen table with a bowl of cereal in front of him and a *talk to me and I'll kill you* expression on his chiseled face. I slid onto the chair next to him, poured myself a bowl of cereal, and listened to Mr. Barrett and Charolette mumble about something in Charolette's room.

Ares snatched the cereal box from me and poured himself a big bowl until there was none left. "What happened?" he asked Marcel.

Marcel growled at him, refusing to make eye contact, and stuffed a spoonful of cereal between his lips. Ares sat across from me and didn't push the matter. Dark circles lay under his dulling eyes, and I wouldn't be surprised if I looked even worse.

I had been awake all night, worrying about his nightmares, and then I'd fucking had one.

After we sat in silence for a few more moments, hearing nothing but incoherent chatter from the other room and the birds chirping outside the window, Mr. Barrett walked into the kitchen with glossy, bloodshot eyes. He gave me a weak smile and sat in the only empty chair, slumping down and thrusting his head into his hands, defeated.

Charolette walked into the kitchen and rubbed her hands together. "I ... I have to tell you and Aurora something, Ares."

Ares glanced over at her with his lips pressed together. "What?"

"I'm officially stopping my chemo treatments and starting hospice early next week."

My heart dropped, and tears welled up in my eyes. I had known that this was coming; she'd warned me yesterday. But it still hurt worse than Nyx's talons had in my neck during that horrid dream last night.

Without finishing his cereal, Marcel stormed out of the room, shaking his head from side to side. Ares sat across from me, completely still, with dead eyes, and something between a grimace and a frown on his lips.

The words had broken him.

Charolette stared at him with watery eyes. "I'm sorry. I just—"

Before she could finish her sentence, Ares pushed his bowl forward and walked out of the room, slammed the front door closed, and disappeared somewhere in the woods. Charolette stared at the door, where both the guys she loved had walked right out to deal with their pain and anger because they were incapable of showing their emotions.

"I didn't want this," Charolette said between sniffles, burying her face into her hands and crying. "I don't want them to hate me for ... for not wanting to suffer anymore. I can't live like this. Can't they see that?"

Mr. Barrett gently rubbed her shoulder and grimaced at me with so much pain in his eyes. First his mate had died, then Mars, and now, his daughter would pass on to the afterlife too soon. And when she did, Ares would go off the rails.

"Go," I whispered to him. "I want to talk to Charolette."

After giving me a thankful half-smile, he walked out the front door.

I gathered Charolette in my arms and pulled her closer to me. "They're sad and in pain. They don't hate you for this decision. They don't think less of you for wanting to stop treatments. It might take them a bit to come around to the idea of hospice, but ... they will. They will want you to have a happy rest of your life. You deserve it."

She sucked her bottom lip into her mouth. "I ... I'm afraid that they'll both go crazy, hurt so much that something is going to happen, and they won't think with their brains during this war because of my decisions."

I pushed some blonde hair out of her face. "I'll talk to them."

Moments passed. Tears still ran down her face. She clutched

onto me. "I love Marcel so much … I love him so freaking much. Out of everyone here, I don't want him to hate me for it the most. He's my mate, Aurora, the only man who loves every part of me."

"He doesn't hate you," I whispered, walking with her to her and Marcel's bedroom and sitting on her bed with her. Sunlight flooded into the room through the orange curtains. "He loves you too. I can see it on his face every time he looks at you."

After wiping some tears from her cheeks with the back of her hand, she crawled back into her bed and pulled the blankets over her eyes, shielding herself from the sun and from all this pain. "Please go talk to him. I've tried all night."

Deciding that she had completely locked out the world, I shut her bedroom door behind me and walked down to the front door, determined to chat with Marcel and Ares about this. They were hurting, but so was she. And Charolette was the one going through all this pain every day. She had the right to be upset.

When I opened the front door, Marcel stood on the porch with his arms crossed over his chest and silver strands of hair blowing into his face, staring out into the dense forest. As soon as I stepped out, the angry, annoyed asshole of a man wrapped his arms around me tightly, taking me by surprise.

"I don't want it to be true," he whispered, his head buried into the crook of my neck.

My eyes widened, and I hesitantly wrapped my arms around him to hug him. This wasn't the Marcel I knew … this was the broken Marcel, the loving Marcel, the Marcel who would do anything for the woman he loved.

It was the Marcel who would agree to Hella's terms.

"I might have a solution," I said, gently patting his back. "But you can't tell anyone about it, especially not Charolette because she would never agree to it."

Marcel tensed and pulled back. "What is it?"

"I don't know if it would work for sure, but Medusa mentioned that Hella had traded lives before. Someone came to her a long time ago, asking to give his life to spend in the underworld for the person he loved to be healthy for a few more years. Hella accepted his request." I paused. "I know I'm asking for a lot, but ..."

"But it could work," Marcel finished. His chin quivered, but he nodded as if he didn't even have to think about giving his life for hers. "If it could work, I'll try it. Anything to keep her happy, healthy, and alive even if that means that I won't be there with her, and as long as Charolette never finds out about it. She would hate me."

"Please, think about it before you agree," I said, glancing around the forest to make sure nobody was listening in on our conversation. "We need you for this war, but if we can have you under Hella's rule, you might be able to get insider information for us ... or she might try to turn you to the wrong side. We need to be careful."

CHAPTER 19

ARES

 *uck.*
Fuck.
Fuck!

I ripped my claws into a tree and tore a fistful of bark right from it, hurling it into the lake. With a loud *thunk*, the bark sank into the water and forced the lake to ripple out. Thrusting my claws into the tree again, I hurled another piece.

And another.

And another.

And even another.

Fuck, I fucking hated feeling this helpless. Charolette was stopping treatments and starting hospice next week. Nothing was working. I had tried everything under the sun, every stupid idea my fucked up head could think up. And still, it had come to this.

Pacing in front of the water, I shook my head and ran my hand through my hair. This couldn't be how it ended for Charolette. I couldn't watch her shrivel away, bruise every time someone touched her, and then die a slow death.

No.

Rage bubbled inside me, my stomach twisting into tight knots that would never truly disappear. I hadn't tried hard enough to help Charolette. I couldn't protect her, too, like Mars had wanted. I'd failed my family.

A failure.

A helpless and hopeless failure.

A bitch of a man.

A fucking brute who couldn't do shit.

That was all I was.

To Mars. To Charolette. To Aurora. To our unborn baby.

And no matter how hard I tried, that was all I would ever be.

CHAPTER 20

AURORA

*A*res wasn't on pack grounds.

I checked the training field, the forest, and even the town.

Desperate to ensure he was okay, I hurried through the forest and toward the lake, where I'd met him that midsummer night. Taking my secret path around the mountain and through a cave, lugging around my pregnant-ass belly, I walked into the clearing right before the sparkling lagoon and found him sitting on a patch of grass, tossing rocks into the lake and tugging on the ends of his hair so hard that I thought he'd rip them out of his head.

A harsh wind whipped through the forest, sending tree branches scraping against one another and rustling wildly above us. I sucked in a breath and walked toward him, watching his shirt ripple against his broad frame.

"Ares," I whispered, crouching down behind him and wrapping my arms around his shoulders. "Ares, tell me you're okay."

Ares stared out at the lake, slumped his shoulders forward, and sighed. "I knew that this was coming, but I couldn't fucking admit it to myself. I have tried everything to make her happy and healthy. Nothing has worked."

Instead of telling him that everything was fine—because I knew it wasn't—I crawled into his arms and brushed some of his thick brown hair out of his face. "You know that I'll be here with you until the very end," I said, staring into those big brown eyes that made me warm in all the right places, "through everything."

He rested his hands on my waist and curled his fingers into my skin. "I know."

And while he acted like everything was okay, his cruel expression told me that this was killing him on the inside. But the god of war would never, ever admit such a thing aloud, especially not when Mars was gone and he thought he had to be strong twenty-four hours a day, seven days a week.

"You remember this place, don't you?" he asked me.

"Of course I do," I said, wanting to tease him to see his fiery eyes again. I hated seeing all this hopelessness inside of them recently. A war had been stirring in his head, one that even I didn't know I could stop. So, I crawled my fingers up his chest and smirked. "I used to meet Tony here all the time."

He growled against my mouth and sucked my bottom lip between his teeth. "Don't play with me like that, Kitten."

"Or what?" I asked, wiggling out of his lap.

Grasping my hips and holding me down to him, he made me straddle his waist. "You're not going anywhere."

"And what are you going to do if I end up slipping away?"

Releasing his hold on me, he smirked, but it didn't reach his eyes. "Try it. See what happens," he dared.

I stared at him for a few moments, lips curling into a smile, and sprinted away from him. I didn't even make it past the lake before Ares wrapped his rough hand around my throat from behind and pushed me against the nearest tree.

He growled into my ear, "I'd chase you to the ends of the earth, Kitten, just to have you."

There was that unruly alpha, who didn't take anyone's shit, that I had fallen in love with.

He turned me around, so I was looking at him, and he maneuvered himself between my legs, burying his face into the crook of my neck and drawing his tongue against his mark. I relaxed against the coarse bark and let out a soft moan, feeling his fingers slip between my legs.

Dipping my fingers underneath his white V-neck, I ran my fingers down his thick abdomen, then his V-line, and grabbed his belt, undoing it and thrusting my hand into his pants. My pussy clenched even harder when I grasped his cock in my hand, stroking it slowly.

"Goddess, Ares," I whispered.

Ares didn't talk about his feelings—ever. He worked through things physically.

I had seen it more than once—with the hounds and with me in bed. If Ares wasn't going to talk to me about what hurt him, then the least I could do was help him relieve his stress a bit, right? I couldn't let him suffer endlessly like this.

He rubbed his fingers against my shorts and laid his canines against my neck again, biting down slightly. "I'm going to take you here like I should've done the first night I met you," he said, slipping a finger into my panties and down my folds.

Wanting him to relax, I pulled off his pants and knelt in the middle of the forest.

The sunrays glowed from behind him, creating dark shadows on his sculpted face. In the pit of darkness, two hungry golden eyes gazed down upon me. He grasped my chin and roughly stroked my jaw.

"Last time, you kept me up all night in the forest, touching my aching pussy," I said, wrapping my hand around the base of his cock and staring up at him through my lashes. I dipped my head and let my tongue glide over his balls, sucking one into my mouth while I stroked his cock. "This time ... it's my turn."

He stiffened and laced a hand in my hair. "Take them both, Kitten."

I sucked his other ball in my mouth at the same time, my tongue lapping against them. He tugged me even closer to him and grunted, resting one hand against the tree bark behind me, his canines growing in his mouth.

"Look at me, Aurora."

Staring up into his golden eyes, I worked my way up his cock, licking and sucking on his shaft and tasting every bit of him. When I reached his head, I swirled my tongue around it and sucked it into my mouth, bobbing my head. I thrust a hand between my legs and slowly teased my clit with my fingers, rubbing it in small and tortuous circles.

"Face-fuck me until you come," I murmured against him. "Please."

"No." Ares curled his lips into a smile and drew a finger down the column of my throat. "I want you to show me how you choke on my cock all by yourself, Kitten. I want to see those eyes fill with tears and spit rolling down your chin because you love it so fucking much."

My pussy clenched. I closed my lips around him and took him until his cock slammed against the back of my throat and my mouth was packed with his shaft. I wrapped one of my hands around my neck and squeezed tightly, feeling him inside me.

When he groaned from the pressure, I bobbed my head back and forth on him for as long, as quickly, and as hard as I could, making sure he reached midway down my throat every time and giving it a good squeeze when he did.

"Fuck, Kitten." He curled his fingers into my hair. "Come all over your fingers for me."

I thrust a finger inside of me, in and out and in and out at the same pace I face-fucked myself with his enormous cock, and parted my lips, moaning on him when I came. Almost immediately, his cum shot against the back of my throat and slid down it.

Not expecting it, I gagged on his dick and went to pull away, yet he pulled me closer to his hips. Spit dripped from my mouth. Tears formed in my eyes. I swallowed his cum and slowly pulled my head back.

When he moved back, I doubled over on the ground, posted my hands on the grass, and gasped for air. Ares knelt down beside me, grabbed my juice-covered fingers, and stuck them into his mouth.

"Let's get home," he finally said, picking me up and setting me on my feet.

And while those eyes had turned godly only a few moments ago, they were back to being filled with nothing but sorrow.

CHAPTER 21

ARES

*A*fter returning home with me, Aurora prepared to leave me to meet Medusa. We were another step closer to stopping this war once and for all and finally building a strong life for our baby, but I didn't want her to leave.

Not after learning that Charolette had decided to stop treatments.

"Don't go, Kitten," I pleaded, wanting her to wait until I finished practice at least. I grabbed her hand and led her to the training area, where all the other wolves were already sparring, including Marcel. "Train with me. You need it as much as I do."

While I would drop practice to go with her, I needed to fucking get all this anger out somehow today and wouldn't have time to train later with anyone. If we were going to the underworld, I needed to be as strong as I could be.

Aurora did too.

"My belly has grown so much over the past few days. I can't go as hard as everyone else," Aurora said. "And if I can't train to my full capacity, then I need you to train while I get us information. Please."

"But," I whispered, stopping my voice from cracking, "I don't want you to go."

Truth fucking was that if Aurora left ...

If she fucking left me, even for a couple hours, I would slip.

I would fucking slip.

I didn't know how much longer I'd be able to keep this facade up. I wasn't okay, and I couldn't say anything to anyone. This entire pack, even Aurora, was counting on me to stay strong. But my mind was tearing me apart.

What if Aurora met Medusa and never came back? What if someone hurt her?

What if, what if, what if ...

The questions didn't stop. The worry wouldn't stop.

It never ended.

She couldn't leave.

"You know that I need to go meet Medusa," Aurora said. "We have questions."

"Wait until practice is over, so I can go with you."

"No." Aurora zipped up her jacket and ran her hand along her bump. "Medusa told me to meet her at this time. She can't wait around all day. We need this information as much as you need to train to be strong and prepared for *us*."

Feeling both fury and sorrow rushing through me, I looked down at her belly, where our pup grew, and nodded. She was going to go whether I wanted her to or not. She was going to leave me alone after this morning. She wanted me to get strong.

But how could I become stronger when I couldn't even control my own thoughts?

I needed to find a way. Somehow.

"I need to protect you, Aurora," I said, anguish in every one of my words.

Part of me didn't even recognize my own voice anymore.

Mars had always been the emotional half of us, not me. And now, I both looked and sounded so weak, even to my fucking mate. I just … I didn't want to carry around the weight anymore.

"Go," I said. "I'll stay and train, so I can protect you this time."

She furrowed her brows. "This time? You've protected me every time we've faced hounds."

She was lying.

"I couldn't protect you during the hound attack last time," I said, wanting to tell her more, desperate for her to stay. Just a bit longer, just a tiny bit longer.

She couldn't leave me so quickly. She couldn't go.

As soon as she walked off this property, the darkness would close in on me. It had been so close to consuming every part of me whenever I wasn't with her, especially after Mars died. If she left …

She stood on her toes and kissed me. "I love you. I'll be back soon."

I gave her my best smile, told her that everything would be okay here, and watched her run off into the Sanguine Wilds to meet Medusa. But when her scent disappeared from the air around me, a heavy, unseen weight crushed my chest.

Nothing was okay.

Everything had been going wrong lately.

I was breaking.

CHAPTER 22

AURORA

*M*edusa stood outside the cave and tugged her veil back when she realized I had come alone. "I must be quick, Aurora. I have business with other gods, but I know you want to talk. So, please, go on."

I sat on a rock inside the cave, breathing in the foul scent of the abandoned hound hideout underneath the dirt ground and remembering when this spot hadn't brought back such horrific memories.

This used to be Jeremy's and my spot.

One day, I would make sure that it was again.

But first, I needed answers about the hounds and the under-world, my powers, and these gods who seemed to plague my dreams and nightmares. Who really was Dawn, and why was I seeing her memories if she was dead?

"Aurora?" Medusa asked, sitting beside me and patting my knee. A soft wind was carried into the cave, her veil blowing gently against my shoulder. "I know that what you've learned these past few weeks is a lot to take in, but I need you to be quick."

Knowing I didn't have much time, I let out a breath. "Can you explain to me how I could heal Elijah but not Charolette again?" I asked, hoping that I could get some ounce of information about why Hella had chosen to take Charolette's life and not Elijah's. "I'm confused about how it all works, and I want answers."

How could I save one but not the other?

Medusa intertwined her fingers and placed her hands on her lap. "You were able to heal Elijah because it was a wound created during a war. All fatal wounds during war are"—she made air quotes—"'overseen' by Morrigan, goddess of war and of death.

"For the most part, she chooses who lives and dies during a battle. Usually, if gods intervene during a war to save a human, she's fairly lenient about giving that human a second chance. Your friend Charolette wasn't wounded during a war, so, long story short, her death is overseen by Hella, who loves torturing lost souls for as long as she can."

"And Marcel could trade his life for Charolette's safety?"

"I said it was a possibility, not a certainty. Nothing is certain with Hella. She's bipolar."

"But I ... I need her to survive," I whispered. "For Ares."

"Ares," she repeated, giving me a small smile, as if she knew something I didn't. After another moment, she patted my knee again, her fingers grazing against my skin. "I will ask around for you, put it out in the world that someone might be interested in striking a deal with Hella."

Again, I couldn't stop myself from wrapping my arms around her and pulling her close. Medusa might be a woman that I barely knew, but she felt more like a mother than Mom had. At least she believed in me and was willing to help me out in any way that she could.

"Now, why were you looking for me at my home, snooping through my journals the other day?" Medusa asked me, shaking her head in disapproval. "You should know not to go into private property. That woman should've taught you better."

That woman? Did she mean Mom?

"I need to find a way to get to the underworld. We are going to bring the fight to the hounds and gods. We can't wait here any longer, or this world will turn into the War of the Lycans, part two. That can't happen, not when I have a baby on the way."

Medusa's eyes widened, and she shook her head. "Don't be stupid, Aurora. The gods in the underworld are stronger than anyone thinks they are. You cannot make the same mistake your brother did. It is what almost killed him."

"My brother is dead because I killed him," I said, my canines aching at the thought.

Sure, the hounds had played a major part in it, but Jeremy had never gone to fight the gods in the underworld. If he had, he would've told me about it or at least mentioned it during our last moments together. Yet all he'd said was that the hounds wanted me for divine revenge.

"No," Medusa said, the snakes restless on her head. "Your brother, Helios."

"Helios is my ... my brother?" I whispered, the entire world slowing down. "How?"

Mom had only given birth twice—once to Jeremy and once to me. And Helios was thousands of years old and a god, for crying out loud. I couldn't be related to him, and I definitely couldn't be his sister.

"Don't play stupid, Aurora. I know that you've figured out that you have divine blood," she said. "But what you don't know is that your soul has been reborn. You've become his sister through divinity—just like Selene, the Moon Goddess, is his sibling."

My eyes widened. "If Selene is my sister and Helios is my brother, then who am I?"

"You, my child, are the goddess of Dawn's soul reborn."

"No way," I whispered.

It was true.

All these memories and dreams that I had been having weren't someone else's, but my own. Ares had been right this entire time; I was a goddess reborn. Yet, still, even as Medusa told me the truth, I couldn't believe it.

I had always been put down, told I wasn't good enough, and shoved to the side.

Now, I was a goddess who reigned over the morning sky.

It was absurd.

"And Ares?" I asked. "What about him?"

"You know who he really is, Aurora."

My heart pounded inside my chest, the quick thump making my wolf go wild. Medusa was right. From the moment that I'd met Ares, I had known who he was. All the stories of him slaughtering packs and ruling wars didn't do him justice.

"Ares is the god of war."

"He is." Medusa nodded. "During the War of the Lycans, he died days after he found your dead body. Overcome with so much rage and violence, he stormed into the underworld, knowing that he would never come back alive. I didn't know it at the time, but he loved you more than anyone could fathom."

A warmth spread through my entire body. Ares had been my lover, even back then.

Even in our past lives, we'd found each other.

"There are no other people in this world who belong together more than you two do."

Grinning from ear to ear, I brushed my fingers against Ares's and then Mars's marks. We belonged together forever, and nobody would ever pull me away from him. Curse Mom and Dad and Tony for trying to rip us apart.

Ares and I were fated in every lifetime.

"You probably have hundreds of questions, so I'll start by answering the question on everyone's mind—how do gods die?"

Medusa started. "To be frank, a god's physical body used to be eternal, thousands of years ago when people were worshipping them constantly. Now, nobody does anymore, and your bodies slowly deteriorate until they are mortal-like. But the souls of divines live on, even when the body can't."

"Is that how this war all started? From Dawn's death?"

"Yes," she continued. "Hella had always fawned over Ares. She wanted him for herself, but he would never give her the time of day. He'd been obsessed with you since the start of time. The only way Hella thought she could have him was by killing you. Not wanting to get her hands dirty, Hella made Nyx murder you."

"Nyx had her own dirty reasons for wanting me dead too," I said. "She wanted Helios to live in the underworld with her."

"You've been seeing visions of it?" Medusa asked.

My cheeks flushed. "Yes, but I might've also read his letter to you in your journal."

Medusa smacked me on the shoulder. "No manners at all. If I'd raised you, you'd know better than that."

"If you'd raised me, I would've had a much better life than what I have now," I said, thinking back to the torture Mom had put me through every single day of my life. Every night, I'd prayed that, one day, I'd wake up, and Mom would be different, but it never happened.

Never.

"Anyway, how do we get to the underworld?" I asked. "If we don't go, this world will turn to chaos, and I refuse to let my daughter grow up in a world where war is the norm. I don't want her to wake up every day, thinking about how she's going to survive. I want her to be at peace."

But now that I'd learned the truth, it was more than just that.

I wouldn't leave Helios down there to fight and die on his own. Any day now, the hounds could reemerge from the underworld and unleash sin and corruption and death over the Sanguine Wilds.

"You cannot go to the underworld. Hella cannot know that you're pregnant."

"We must eliminate the threat before it becomes worse," I said, but deep down, I knew that Medusa was right. I needed to keep my baby a secret from Hella or else she'd try to harm the pup. But she'd still be in harm's way if we didn't try to defeat Hella.

How could I keep my daughter a secret for the rest of her life?

It was a lose-lose situation.

"There's only one way to keep your child safe," Medusa said, as if reading my mind.

"How?" I whispered, drawing a hand over my bump, over-come with so many emotions. My daughter was about to come into this world, and I had no idea how to use my powers to protect her.

Medusa paused and refused to look me in the eye.

"How?" I repeated.

"Give her away," she muttered under her breath.

My heart dropped, and I stood. "No."

Medusa stood beside me, finally looking into my eyes with her green ones. "You must."

With my canines lengthening, I shook my head. "You can't be serious. How can you even suggest something like this? Ares and I *need* our baby. We can't deal with any more loss. We are not giving her away to anyone."

"Stop thinking about yourself, Aurora," Medusa snapped, nostrils flaring. "You want a good life for your daughter. You are in this war whether you want to be or not. You need to think about her in all of this."

"How could you suggest this?" I asked again, my voice barely above a whisper.

There was no way I'd ever give up my baby girl. I had grown her in my belly for so long. Ares and I ... couldn't lose someone else. Mars's wish was for us to be a family together, and I couldn't fulfill that if she wasn't with me.

And besides, I refused to let someone else raise my daughter. My parents were shit, and I wanted to make sure that our little girl had a good upbringing, one that I only wished that I'd had.

For years, I had wished that Mom and Dad really loved and cared about me. There wasn't a way I could leave my daughter here to grow up with someone who acted as her parents when Ares and I were perfectly capable.

My chest tightened. But how was I going to keep her safe in the underworld? If I didn't give birth before then, Hella would aim to slaughter my baby before she could ever take her first breath.

Fuck being a goddess.

This shit was too hard already.

Medusa cleared her throat, clasped her hands together, and gazed emptily at her feet. "You know, when I was younger, I gave up my daughter, so she could grow up in a safe environment. At least, safer than being with me."

And suddenly, I retracted all thoughts that I'd had earlier of Medusa being a motherly figure. I looked at her, furrowing my eyebrows and wondering how she could have done that. If someone had been trying to get pregnant for so long with the person that they loved and they had a stable home for them, how could they give their child up?

"How do you give up someone you're supposed to love with your entire heart?" I asked. "Don't you live every day, wondering how she's doing or if she's safe? Do you ever wonder if she'd ever look at you and just know who you really were to her?"

"I think about it every day and remind myself that, even if I never see her again or if she has no idea who I am, I still love her." Medusa shuffled her feet against the dirt. "I didn't even allow myself to have an hour with her before I gave her away. I didn't get to see the first time she smiled or hear her first laugh or ... I didn't even let her tiny hands touch my face."

"Then, why?" I whispered, tears quickly running down my cheeks. "Why give her up?"

"Because the choice I made for her was the best one at the time. It was damn hard, not seeing her grow up, but I knew that she was safe and that she had a strong family protecting her every day of her life."

Turning away from her, I rested my hands on my belly, and stared into the Sanguine Wilds. "I will not give my child away."

Our pup would already be growing up without Mars. I refused to let her grow up without Ares and me too. We were her fucking parents, and nobody—not even the woman who had given up her baby for the greater good—was going to sway my decision.

"Think about it," Medusa said, walking next to me. "It will be the hardest decision of your life, but you will thank me for it. You will know that your pup is safe. In the meantime, I will try to find you an undercover way to the underworld."

CHAPTER 23

ARES

*W*here is Aurora? Where the fuck is she?

I paced back and forth in our bedroom, my thoughts racing through my head at lightning fucking speed. I should've never let Aurora go by herself to that cave. For the first time since that hound attack, we were separated by more than a couple blocks.

She was somewhere deep in the forest, where I couldn't protect her.

And I had let her go.

I'd fucking let her go.

How could I ever protect her and our baby? All those dreams last night—every night since Mars had died—proved one thing and one thing only. Throughout my lifetimes, I hadn't been able to protect Aurora once. What would make this time any different?

The god of war was nothing but weak, frail, and powerless.

Aurora deserved more than me. I could offer her nothing.

With Charolette dying, Mars gone, and my fucking control slipping, I ... I dug my claws into my palms and closed my eyes at the feel of pain. At first, this felt like what I deserved. But then relief flooded through my body, something I couldn't quite explain. For a moment, everything was peaceful again, and all I could focus on was the slight, dull pain on my palms.

I wanted it to stop.

I wanted the hurt to stop, the anxiety to stop, the nightmares to stop.

Pain had always been the only way to bring me back down to reality. It was the only thing that I could control before the horrid thoughts and memories, nightmares and dreams flooded my mind once more.

And in an instant, all that pain was back and so loud that I couldn't think straight.

I'm not good enough. I can never protect Aurora. Our baby will die along with her.

Weak.

A weak man.

I am a weak fucking man who can't do anything fucking right.

I let Aurora walk through the forest alone.

I let her fucking go.

Staring at myself in the bathroom mirror, I shook my head at how weak I looked.

A man with tears in his eyes. A man with scars that didn't heal. A man with pain.

It felt like the agony of a hundred thousand warriors howling and dying in battle. The thoughts never stopped. The pain never stopped. The insecurities never stopped. No matter how fucking hard I tried to get them to go away.

After splashing some water on my face to try to think clearly, I growled louder than I ever had and slammed my fist into the bathroom mirror. The bloody glass clattered into the sink. Some broken pieces still attached to the wall were cracked in all directions.

Snatching a large piece of glass in my palm, I let my skin tear to shreds against the sharp edges. My sister was dying. I couldn't protect Mars. I would never be able to protect my family from the hurt. There was too much of it, too fucking much.

A tear slid down my cheek. I'd never be a good father.

All the little white scars on my forearms were reminders of how weak I really was.

I wasn't a strong god. I was just a weak wolf.

I pushed a piece of glass against my forearm and let it sink deep. The blood trickled from the small incision. Weak. I was so weak. I didn't deserve Aurora. I had lost her once already, and I would lose her again.

It seemed we had always been a secret, never able to be truly together. But now, we were, and I loved her with my entire heart. There was no way—no fucking way—I could lose her. I needed my control back.

Everything was so loud.

All I could see was her eyes staring back at me in the cracked mirror, her once-lively eyes so dull and dead.

Deeper. I pushed the glass deeper until I felt like I could breathe again.

My shoulders slumped forward, and I watched bead after bead of blood drip into the white sink. I rested my forearm against the counter and took a huge breath of air. Everything was calm again, calmer than it had been since the night of the Luna Ceremony when I pulled Aurora close and kissed her for the first time as my luna.

This was what I needed.

This was the only thing that helped me think straight anymore.

I fucking loved Aurora so much. I had to do this for her.

CHAPTER 24

AURORA

*W*ith trembling hands, I opened the front door and stepped into the eerily quiet pack house. Ruffles met me in the foyer with her eyes wide and her fur raised, as if she was scared or nervous, and then she meowed and looked up the stairs.

I pet her backside, pushing her fur back into place, and blew out a deep breath.

How would we keep our baby girl alive when we traveled to the underworld? We barely had a plan on how to defeat Hella, and we had absolutely no idea what the underworld looked like or how it worked. When we got there, everything could be different from what we thought it was.

Tears formed in my eyes, but I pushed them away and ran a hand over my belly bump. If Ares saw me crying, he'd ask what happened with Medusa, and I didn't have the heart to tell him what she had suggested.

Especially not after what Charolette had admitted earlier.

"Meow," Ruffles said, pushing her head into the back of my calf and toward the stairs.

Hazelnut drifted through the house from our bedroom. I inhaled Ares's scent deeply, letting my shoulders slump forward and relaxing only slightly. When Ruffles meowed again, I walked up the stairs to our bedroom and smiled softly to myself.

Thank the goddess that I was mated to that man.

Even when I was a wreck, he could always calm me down.

Stepping into our bedroom, I found Ares standing over the sink in our connected bathroom. I walked over, peeked my head into it, and stopped dead in my tracks, tears welling up in my eyes. "Ares, what are you doing?!"

Blood ran down the sides of the white sink bowl, dripping from above. The mirror was shattered into a thousand tiny pieces, littered on the floor and in the sink too. Ares's body was violently heaving up and down.

He turned around in shock with a large piece of glass lodged into his forearm, deep enough to leave a scar, even on an alpha who had superior healing abilities. When Ares saw me, he pulled it out of his flesh, as if he didn't want me to see, but it was too late.

Tears immediately poured down my cheeks. My heart pounded in my ears.

"Ares!" I sobbed. "Ares, why?"

I wiped the tears with the backs of my hands, but they continued to cloud my vision. I wanted to both hug him and slap him, scream at him for ever doing that to himself and tell him that I would always be there for him, no matter what.

But, Goddess, I didn't know what to do.

Knowing that Ares had cut himself in the past was one thing. It was another to see the man I loved forcing himself to hurt and bleed in private because he couldn't deal with the pain anymore.

"Aurora, I'm sorry," he said, dropping the glass.

The bloody edges clattered against the sink counter, the blood splattering in the bowl. My gaze landed back on his forearm and on the huge gash in it that wasn't healing. He placed a hand over the wound, so I couldn't see it.

"Please, don't hate me."

I parted my lips to speak, to say something, anything, but I couldn't. After Medusa had told me to give away my pup to now coming home to see my mate hurting himself, it was almost too much to handle.

Ares stepped closer to me, and I had the urge to move back, but I stopped myself and stared up into his wide, wavering gaze. Tears filled his wide brown eyes, and he grabbed my hands.

"You weren't supposed to see that. I'm sorry. Don't hate me," he repeated again.

Trembling, I walked past him into the bathroom, grabbed the closest towel, and pressed it against his wounds, my fingers shaking as I clamped it around his forearm. Blood stained the towel, drenching right through it, and I bit back another sob.

"Aurora, talk to me, please," he said.

Yet I couldn't look him in the eye.

I didn't want him to see my hurt and sorrow—from not only what Medusa had told me, but also from my mate harming himself again. This was my fault for not knowing that this was how he felt. If I had focused on him a bit more or asked the therapist to come over more often, I could've done something to stop this.

Fuck, I should've been here.

I should've never left to talk to Medusa.

"Sit down," I whispered, voice shaking, nodding to the toilet. "Please."

Ares sat immediately. I turned toward the sink to wet the towel and gasped when I saw the sheer amount of blood in the bowl. I clutched onto the counter, nearly doubling over at the sight of it, and blinked away tears.

While I had seen more blood before, I hadn't seen anything like this.

Ares stood. "Aurora."

"Sit back down," I said to him, not wanting *him* to comfort *me*.

I should've been able to hold myself together for him. He was the one hurting.

"Aurora," Ares said again.

I turned on my heel toward him and pointed a sharp claw at the toilet. "Sit," I said strongly, not letting my voice waver this time. It had come out too harsh—I knew that it had—but I couldn't help it.

After Ares sat, I turned on the sink and let the water wash away the blood in the bowl. I pushed the towel under the rushing warm water and then turned back to Ares. I still couldn't look him in the eye as I knelt in front of him and grasped his wrist.

As I wiped away the blood from his forearm, I stared down at every old and new scar on his skin. My lips trembled, but I vowed to stay strong and finish cleaning all the blood before I broke down into more unruly tears.

He tucked a strand of hair behind my ear. "I'm sorry, Kitten. I'm so sorry."

My fingers dug into his skin, and I finally looked up at him through watery eyes. I grasped his face in my hands, promising myself to be strong. "Don't apologize. I told you that I'm going to be here with you through everything, Ares," I whispered through the tears. "You're not alone in this. You don't have anything to be sorry for."

Ares stayed quiet for a few moments and then doubled over, his entire body collapsing in on itself. He stared at me with trembling eyes, all his walls finally shattering. "There is a war going on in my fucking head, Aurora. And it never stops." His voice broke. "It never fucking stops."

"You don't have to keep it all in," I whispered, pushing some hair off his sweaty forehead. "Talk to me about it. Tell me every-

139

thing that makes you hurt. I'm here with you forever, Ares, and I won't ever leave you."

Ares enveloped me in a hug for a long time, just resting his head on my shoulder. When he finally calmed his breathing, he picked me up and placed me on the sink counter, standing between my legs. And even then, he held me close to him.

I ran my fingers across his back and laid my head on his shoulder, staring at his sculpted face.

After forty minutes of holding him, I lifted my head and brushed some hair out of his face. "We need to talk about Medusa. She had a lot to say when I met her earlier."

"Go ahead," Ares said, voice gruff.

While she had told me so much, I didn't even know where to start. This was so much—almost too much—to pile on Ares's shoulders, but he needed to know now. The war was here, whether we wanted it or not.

We needed to survive.

"We are gods. Medusa told me herself. During the War of the Lycans, I died, and you died shortly after. Our souls were reborn into these bodies. She will find us a way to the underworld," I said. "And she'll put in a word about Marcel taking the place of Charolette's life. Though I do hope that Hella doesn't think this is a trap. With Marcel in the underworld and under her control, we'll have him feed us information about what's going on—as long as he doesn't break and let Hella control him."

"Charolette can be saved?" Ares asked, eyes widening.

"But we'll lose Marcel."

Ares stared down at the bathroom floor. "Marcel is strong and is her mate. He'll do whatever we require him to do and get whatever kind of information that we need from Hella in order to destroy her."

"Is that it?" I whispered.

He doesn't have any other questions about Medusa telling us we are gods?

Rocking forward, he glanced between us for a quick moment. "I actually have something to admit to you. I've been having visions of the past. Every night, I see you die, Aurora. Every fucking night, I watch you reach out for me as someone kills you. I don't think I'll be strong enough to protect you and our baby."

Visions? Just like mine, I suppose.

"You will protect her," I told Ares, grabbing his hands and placing them on my stomach. "And no matter what happens, no matter how hard life gets for us, no matter how much you think that you won't be enough, remember that we created her. She's ours. She will grow up, knowing how strong and protective you are of her, even before she was ever born."

Ares rubbed the scar on his chest. "In all those past lives, we could never be together. We were always hiding our relationship from someone or something. This life ... I finally have you, and I can't let you go."

After a long few moments of silence, I cleared my throat. "But we have to think about her in all of this too," I said, glancing at the sink and frowning.

There was no way that I could tell him about Medusa suggesting that I give the baby away, not after what I had just seen him do. He needed this baby just as much as I did.

"I'm going to give birth anytime now. Our baby is getting bigger and stronger by the day, and she has grown far faster than a wolf does. We can't bring her to the underworld, and I can't go like this."

Ares paused. "What are you saying?"

I shrugged my shoulders. "We just have to prepare."

"You're saying to give her away, aren't you?" he asked me, staring me deep in my eyes with nothing but pain and anguish. His top lip twitched—in disgust or anger, I didn't know. I couldn't quite tell how he felt about it.

"No," I said to him honestly. "I can't give her away. I need her."

After Mom, Dad, Jeremy, and Mars, I couldn't lose anyone else.

"I can go to the underworld alone," Ares said.

"No."

If I let him go down there alone, he might not ever come back up, just like Helios. If Helios was as strong as Medusa had made him out to be, I didn't know if Ares would be strong enough to handle it alone down there for so long without me.

Ares grasped my chin in his hand. "Then, what do you suggest we do?"

My gaze drifted to him and then to the bare wall behind him. There wasn't a way that we could win. If we brought our girl to the underworld, Hella would try to kill her. If Ares left for the underworld by himself, I might never see him again, and this war might never end. If we left her up here … maybe we could stop the war soon, so she could live safely.

"I'd rather you stay here," he finally said. "That way, I know you're safe. Every other time you've been at war with me, you always end up dying, and I can never protect you from those evils. If you come with me, I'm fucking terrified that this time, it won't be any different. I won't be able to protect you or her."

I rested my hands on his chest, curling my fingers into the thick muscle. "I'm not leaving you. This time *is* different. You said it yourself," I whispered, brushing some hair from his forehead. "This time, we get to finally be together, stand together, and fight together. And when we're together, nobody can stop us."

CHAPTER 25

ARES

"*D*enise will be here in five minutes," Aurora said from the doorway.

I stared up at the ceiling and blew out a breath, jaw tight so it wouldn't quiver. "Why?"

Aurora took a hesitant step into the room and fiddled with the rings on her finger. "Because you need to get better. If you could just listen to Denise and hear her out, then maybe ... maybe you can clear your mind of some of these ... worries."

After vowing not to blow up at Aurora, I nodded and rolled off the bed to find a shirt in my dresser. It wasn't Aurora's fault that my head had been fucking shit lately, but still, I fucking loathed Denise. I didn't want her prying.

Grasping my face, Aurora stared up at me through watery eyes. "I just want you to be healthy and ... happy again. I want my strong, *don't give a fuck* Ares back to help me save the world and kill hounds."

I placed my hands over hers, leaned into her touch, and closed my eyes, warmth spreading throughout my chest. "I'm sorry that I'm so fucked up, Aurora. You deserve someone who's there for you, no matter what."

"Stop it," she scolded, the skin between her brows creasing. "*You* are that man. *You* are who I deserve. *You* are going to go into that therapy session with Denise and talk for the sake of me and our pup, who is going to look up to you one day with so much love in her eyes. And you're going to thank yourself for surviving."

Tears pricked the corners of my eyes. "Okay."

Someone knocked on the front door, and Aurora gave me a reassuring smile. "It'll be okay. You're going to get better, Ares. This is just the first step." When she pulled away, she guided me down the hallway to the living room, where Marcel had let in Denise.

As I walked by her, Charolette stared at me through teary eyes and inched closer to Marcel, burying her face into his chest and letting out an unruly sob. She always hated it the most that I harmed myself. By falling back into it, I'd let her down too.

"Come on, Charolette," Marcel said, walking her down the stairs and out the front door to give us privacy.

The door slammed closed from the wind, and my heart pounded hard. I didn't want to be here, but I had to do this for Aurora.

Aurora ushered me to the couch. "Sit down. I'm going to step away for a bit."

When her fingers left mine and she walked away from me, a chill rolled through my entire body. I would get better for her, no matter fucking what. I would never let that woman walk out of my life because she couldn't deal with this fucking sickness.

"Ares," Denise said. "How are you feeling?"

"Fine," I snapped.

But then I remembered the look on Aurora's face when she'd walked in on me.

"I'm not fine," I whispered, slumping my shoulders forward and finally letting go, really giving it a try this time.

If Mars had liked this woman, she couldn't be that bad, right? He must've trusted her enough to let her in on our secrets.

Tears welled in my eyes. "I'm really not fine."

Denise leaned forward and grasped my hand. "That's okay, Ares. I'm here to help you. Let's finally fix this, not only for you or for Aurora, but also for your baby on the way. I'm going to give you the tips and tools you need to find yourself again."

CHAPTER 26

AURORA

"$\mathcal{E}$lijah," I whispered, stepping onto the porch.

He leaned against the porch, staring out into the dark Sanguine Wilds. I thrust my arms around him, buried my face into his chest, and sobbed. Since I'd found Ares cutting himself, I'd wanted to cry my eyes out, but I'd held it in for the sake of Ares.

Yet I couldn't anymore.

This was so damn hard.

Like a big brother, Elijah wrapped his arms around me and hugged me close to him, rocking us back and forth and gently stroking my hair. "I'm so sorry, Aurora. I'm so, so sorry. You should've never had to walk in on something like that."

Tears poured down my cheeks, and I hiccuped. "If he keeps this up, I'm afraid that I'm … I'm going to … to lose him. He's going to spiral out of control and slip into the darkness for good, Elijah."

"Shh, shh, shh."

I dug my fingers into his shoulders and cried harder. "There was so much blood."

Maybe it was wrong to tell Elijah about Ares. But I didn't have anyone to talk to about it. Between this and Hella and the hounds constantly attacking, I had the entire damn world on my shoulders.

It was hard—so frustratingly hard—to be the person who made sure everyone was okay, the person who everyone looked up to for plans about the future. Ever since Mars had died, Ares had nearly checked out. It always had to be me.

And I ... I couldn't do this alone anymore.

I doubled over into Elijah's arms, my knees collapsing. "You don't understand how much it upsets me to see the man I love want to hurt himself all the time. He's desperate and lonely, and he can't deal without being with Mars," I whispered. "It's breaking my heart."

Elijah rubbed my back and let me cry into his shirt. He didn't tell me that it was okay.

If he had, I wouldn't have believed him.

This wasn't okay in the slightest.

"I know how it feels," Elijah said after moments of complete silence. "Jeremy begged to die, didn't he? He didn't want to be in this world anymore because of all the horrors in it, his quality of life ..." When he pulled away, he had tears in his eyes. "When he died the second time, I felt like it was my fault. I should've been there with him all those years. I should've protected him. I should've been the one to help him through it all—hound or human."

My chest tightened at the thought of Jeremy being gone and what Elijah must've gone through. I should've asked him more about it, made sure he was getting along okay with all the pain. Yet I had been numb at the time myself—too numb to think straight.

"You can't blame yourself," Elijah said. "No matter how much you want to. You can't. You couldn't have been with Ares during all those years that screwed him up. You can't protect him from the past and everything that has come about because of it. All you can do is love him and let him know that you're with him, no matter what."

"It's just damn hard," I admitted, nodding and wiping my cheeks with the backs of my hands and then taking a hesitant seat in one of the rocking chairs. "So damn hard to even think about him wanting to hurt himself and harder to see it happen too."

Elijah sat beside me. "I know," he whispered, placing a hand on my knee and squeezing. "I know it is, but that's life. We can't deal with everyone's problems. We can only deal with our own and love those we care about."

I hugged my knees to my chest. "Love," I whispered finally, a small smile crossing my face at the thought of Ares—the man who I must've loved for thousands of years. "Love is our greatest weakness and our greatest strength. We do stupid things for it, but we wouldn't be who we are without it."

Ares had said he watched me die over and over again in the past—in all the times we could never be together—but this time, we could be so open with our love that I hoped we could make a difference. It had to be a sign, right?

"We're gods, Elijah," I said. "Medusa told me earlier this morning."

"Gods," Elijah repeated. "The gods, Dawn and Ares?"

"How'd you know?" I asked.

He gave me a sheepish smile. "I've been reading about the gods lately, and it seemed like those would be yours with your powers. Dawn is the goddess of the dawn—sister to Helios, the sun god, and Selene, the Moon Goddess. And as we all know, Ares is the god of war. Suits him pretty well still."

I paused for a moment and let it sink in. We had really been gods in past lives.

"They died the last time they fought Hella. From what I read, Dawn had received many wounds from Hella and Nyx that should've been fatal, but only the last one killed her—or killed you."

That explained Ares's visions. He'd said he saw me die many times before, but maybe he had seen others killing me and not my actual death itself. If I had survived all those other wounds and only died while I was chained up in the underworld, it would fit with what Medusa and Helios had said.

Gods suffered near fatal wounds, but only a certain kind of power killed them.

A power that Nyx had.

"But this time," Elijah continued, "is different."

It would be different.

My gaze shifted toward the forest. It would definitely be—

Two glowing indigo eyes stared back at me, accompanied by at least forty yellow-golden ones surrounding it, making the forest a ball of light. My chest tightened, and I stood to my feet.

"Hounds!" I screamed. "The hounds are here!"

Within a moment, the quiet nights we had been granted exploded with growls, teeth, and blood. They attacked from all directions, sprinting at the pack house and toward our warrior wolves that emerged from the forest behind us.

I desperately wanted to move, but I couldn't.

All I could seem to do was stare at those indigo eyes, which hadn't moved yet.

Nyx.

Nyx was here. This was her.

I held one hand over my baby bump and collapsed onto the ground, memories searing through my flesh like a burning heat. Sweat flowed down my back, beads curling around my rib cage and drenching my shirt.

What is happening? Why can't I move?

"Aurora!" Elijah shouted.

"Kill them!" Ares ripped through the front door, transformed into his wolf, and stood over my body, his chest heaving up and down, his canines drawn, and his wounds from earlier still not healed. "*I'll protect Aurora*," he said through the mindlink.

While we had more warriors than hounds, the monstrosities were harder to kill and looked so much stronger. I curled into a ball, clutching my baby and screaming at the top of my lungs. Piercing pain shot through my body so hard that I squeezed my eyes closed, seeing nothing but memories of a past life.

The same memory of my death from last time.

Yet I couldn't stop it.

"LET ME OUT!" I screamed, grasping on the thick divine chains bound to my neck. "Nyx!"

Sitting in a silver cage with rotting corpses, rats, and an over-whelming stench of blood, I curled myself up into a tight ball as Hella stared down at me. Erebus, Nyx's brother, walked down the stone steps with Nyx, the indigo-haired woman.

"Will she do it?" Hella asked Erebus.

Erebus pushed Nyx toward me. "If she wants me to let her roam free one day."

My hands and ankles were bound together so tightly that I couldn't move them. "Nyx! Let me out, please! They're going to torture me down here," I begged the girl, tears streaming down my face.

Erebus pushed her into the cell with me and shut the door behind her. "Tear her to pieces. I want your lover, Helios, to hurt, Nyx. I want him to hate you. I want him to try to come down here and kill you, so you can kill his ass because you're mine, Nyx."

"No, Nyx! Please, don't listen to him," I pleaded with her, swallowing the salty tears as they rolled onto my dry lips. "You can't kill immortals. You can't ..." I whispered.

They had tried killing me so many times, but they couldn't.

"Just let me go. Please, let me go."

Hella laughed right in my face. "Darling, you shouldn't have touched a man who wasn't yours. You are going to get everything you deserve." Hella turned to Nyx. "Make it hurt oh-so good."

"Ares has never been yours!" I shouted. "You can try to kill me, Nyx ... but you won't be able to. No god has died—ever." My heart raced quickly at the sight of her.

She walked toward me with an unreadable expression on her face.

"Not true," Erebus said, lips curled into a smirk. "Nyx killed one just last year. She's the only goddess able to tear another divine to pieces. All those rumors those earthly gods have been whispering about are true. You should've believed them."

Nyx, the goddess of the night, turned to me, her nails lengthening into talons.

I shook my head at her. "It's not true, Nyx. I know you. You're not bad. You're good ..."

"It's true," she said.

Instead of the same memory I had last time, this one changed.

Erebus and Hella walked out of the dingy dungeon, leaving me alone with Nyx.

"I would kill you over and over and over again if it meant I could be with Helios in the underworld," she whispered only to me. "We were never friends because I liked you. We were friends because you were the only one who hid my relationship with Helios from my brother and Hella. They're onto you now, so I need to kill you. No hard feelings."

"No fucking hard feelings?!" I screamed at her. "You're a—"

She dug her fingers into my belly and ripped it apart, as if it were nothing. I screamed, unable to move, and clutched my stomach harder. Last time, she had slashed her talons across my throat, but this time, she continued to rip away at my stomach.

Where my baby was in real life, not in this memory.

My baby!

I clutched my stomach and squeezed my eyes shut, shaking my head from side to side. "You can't have her!"

When the raging stopped, I opened my eyes. Suddenly, the room

changed, and we were standing in complete darkness, as if we were in a
different realm altogether. Nyx had cut her hair shorter and those
indigo eyes looked older, like years of darkness had taken over them.

"I will find you again," Nyx said, glancing down at my belly.

She stepped closer to me and dug her fingers into my stomach again,
and I could do nothing but scream.

"I will kill you to keep Helios down here. He's not leaving the under-
world anymore."

I SLAPPED one hand over my bump and the other onto the
ground, an indescribable power rushing through me and exiting
through my fingers. My belly throbbed, like it was being torn
apart from the inside out. I looked down at it to see the blood
pouring out of it.

Has Nyx physically hurt me in my memories?

"No …" I screamed, pressing my hand to the wound. "No!"

Tears streamed down my face. I used all the might I had left to
close the wounds before anything could happen to my baby.
Lightly—very lightly—I could still feel her inside me, her tiny
little heart beating slightly.

Ares shifted into his human form and knelt by my side.
"Aurora, what's—"

"Don't touch me, Ares," I said, the power and pain swelling
inside of me.

I didn't want to hurt him, and I didn't know how to control
this either.

When he grasped my belly, I screamed, "I said, don't
touch me!"

Overcome with vigor, I struck my hand against the dirt. The
solid ground shook, the hounds flying through the air from the
sheer force of my hand impacting the ground. Their bodies
slammed against the nearest trees, branches digging into
their fur.

"Don't touch me!" I said again, this time staring into the darkness at those indigo eyes.

As if he sensed the power within me, one hound stopped growling at us and *turned* on the other fiends. The haziness that clouded every hound's eyes suddenly faded from his as he looked over at me with some sort of hope or happiness.

I didn't know what I had done to shake away the haze in his eyes or the spell he had been put under. But it must've worked because when the other hounds ran at us again, that hound stood his ground and fought the large ones—the same way that Jeremy had with Fenris—as if he was protecting me.

And before those feral hounds could ever come within feet of us again, he ripped them apart, piece by piece.

CHAPTER 27

AURORA

*O*nce the hound slaughtered the others, he stood before us with sanguine-colored fur and clear, unmurky eyes. After catching his breath, he turned around to face me and approached us slowly. Something about him seemed different than the other hounds that we'd fought before.

He was smaller and looked more like a rogue from earth than a hound from the dead.

Ares lunged at him, but I held him back. "Don't."

"Aurora," Ares said to me through the mindlink. *"Kill him, or I will."*

"No," I said to Ares.

I wanted to see why this lone hound had betrayed the others and protected me. What had he felt when I thrust my hand against the ground and threw him into the air? Was it just a divine power or something else?

As the hound walked closer to us, I knelt down and held out my hand for him. Nerves zipped through me, my hand covered in blood from my stomach and trembling slightly. Memories still drifted through my mind of my past life, and something about this hound seemed so eerily familiar.

When he reached my feet, the hound bowed his head to me, and after a few cautious moments, he pushed his snout into my hand. I drew him closer and let my fingers run down his raggedy coat, coating my fingers in more blood.

"I know you," I whispered.

Sitting back, I placed my hand over my bump and closed my eyes to remember.

I LEANED back in a meadow of flowers, humming to myself and watching the morning sun rise over the trees. A rogue wolf—this wolf—appeared in the distance, walking over to me and resting his head in my lap. I stroked his fur.

Hounds were usually ruthless wolflike beasts—sometimes three-headed, sometimes two, mostly one—with an innate instinct to rip people apart. Some even thought that, under an evil leader, hounds could kill a god.

"Oh, come on, Nyx," I found myself saying, my icy-white hair blowing in the breeze. I let out a giggle. "You know that I know about you and my brother. I hide you two. I can see it in his eyes every time I mention your name. Is it still just flirting, or is there more?"

"Dawn," Nyx said, voice sharp. "Please, not now."

I stroked the wolf's fur and watched him blissfully close his eyes. "Fine, I'll tell you about my love life, whether you want to hear about it or not," I said. "Promise me that you won't tell anyone."

"You know me, Dawn." Nyx smiled at me. "I wouldn't do that."

And so, I dove into my nights with Ares while stroking the rogue's fur, lost in a world of bliss. My cheeks flushed, and I lay on my back. The wolf lay on my stomach, resting his head on my chest and licking my face, like he always did.

I smiled up at him and let my hand run over his fur. He let out a

*long, low howl, and more rogues appeared in the forest, running over to
us. They all lay by my side, their paws sprawled out on my stomach, my
arms, and my legs as they sat with their eyes closed in utter delight.*

I REOPENED my eyes and smiled down at the wolf, love bursting
through my body. It felt like I had the spirit of hundreds of
wolves rushing through me at this very moment, making me
stronger than I'd ever hoped to be.

"You're not a real hound, are you?" I whispered.

The wolf moved closer until his head was pressed against my
forehead. *"No,"* he said through my mind, something I'd never
thought could happen without a mind-link connection. *"I'm a
rogue, brought to the underworld during the War of the Lycans. There
are hundreds down there that they captured. Some of which I had to kill
just now to protect you. My comrades."*

"Hundreds?" I asked, brows furrowed.

*"They're being corrupted with darkness every day. You need to help
us, Dawn. We can't survive down there any longer. We will die down
there if this war continues. We've been waiting for you to come get us."*

Tears welled up in my eyes, feeling the pain he must've felt for
thousands of years.

For a moment, his eyes flashed indigo, and my wolf growled
at the eyes of Nyx—the woman who had promised to kill me
over and over again. He bared his canines and growled almost
internally. I balled my hands into fists, so I wouldn't hurt the
wolf, who had clearly been taken over by Nyx and Hella down in
the underworld.

"They're taking control of our minds and killing our mates," he
managed to say.

Again, his eyes turned indigo for a longer period of time. I
growled at him to stay back because I couldn't control myself
right now. I couldn't kill him. We needed help. He had so much

knowledge of the underworld and the people down there who could aid us.

He growled again—at me this time—eyes flashing back and forth between indigo and gold, an internal war that a hound wouldn't survive against a god.

"Nyx's here. She's—I ... I can't stop h—" Suddenly, he stumbled away and shook his head back and forth, howling. *"Stay away from me ... I didn't do ... stop. Let ... me ... go."*

When his eyes shifted into indigo and never turned back to their lovely gold, he leaped at me with his teeth bared. Pain shot through me, but to protect myself, I reached up and crushed his jaw until the indigo faded.

He touched my baby bump with his paw, and unruly rage ran through my veins. It was Nyx's one last try to destroy my baby tonight, but it didn't work. He slumped against my stomach, his head resting on my belly, like it had during my memory.

"Your baby will be strong," he said to me, light fading from his eyes. *"And Mars has been waiting for her."*

Heart racing, I stroked the wolf's fur as it died slowly in my arms. "Mars?"

He took his last breath. *"Mars is in the underworld too."*

CHAPTER 28

ARES

"*M*ars is alive," Aurora whispered.

My stomach dropped, my chest tightening.

All this time, I had been forcing myself not to believe that he could still be alive. I didn't want to get my, Aurora's, or our pack's hopes up for nothing. But now that I knew he was somewhere in the underworld, wandering around aimlessly, I felt relieved somehow.

This nightmare was coming to an end.

Aurora might've reassured me that I'd be a good father. But what kind of man would I be if I didn't try to find Mars for her and for our pup? I needed to get him back. He deserved to see his baby girl one day. He had sacrificed himself for her.

When the hound fell limp in Aurora's arms, she laid him on the ground and glanced up at me through teary eyes and a wavering smile.

My chest tightened even more, and I drew her up to her feet, wrapping my arms around her shoulders and tugging her close to me. I didn't know how the hell it was possible though. Denise had assured me over and over again that Mars was just dormant. And while I knew it wasn't true, how could he completely split from his body?

Was Mars a walking corpse? A body double?

"He's alive, Ares," Aurora whispered to me, pulling away and grasping my face in her soft hands. She rested her forehead against mine and let happy tears race down her cheeks, her body trembling back and forth slightly. "Alive."

"Maybe," I said. "We don't know anything for sure until we see him again."

Unlike every other time I mentioned Mars, Aurora's smile didn't falter. "There's hope."

"Hope."

I ran my hand over her belly, freezing when my fingers grazed over her ripped shirt. I pulled away slightly, my eyes wide and my worst fears racing through my fucked up head. Had I not been able to completely stop the hounds from touching Aurora? How had she gotten this?

"Nyx," she whispered, curling her fingers around the bottom of her shirt and hesitantly lifting it enough to uncover her huge belly. Completely healed claw marks stretched across her stomach, the fresh scars still red.

"How?" I whispered.

She hadn't been here.

Yet this proved that she must've been lurking somewhere.

"She was inside my head," Aurora said and then pulled down her shirt.

My heart dropped. "What about the baby?"

"I can feel her still," she whispered, gently grasping my hand. "Don't worry."

After letting out a breath of relief, I gulped. "That happened in your mind?"

"I guess so. I don't know what Nyx's capable of. Maybe she was here …"

She placed one hand on her belly bump and the other around my forearm. Not wanting her exposed here for much longer, I ushered her into the house, where Denise stared out the window.

I barked at Marcel through the mind link to have the other alphas meet here first thing in the morning.

We couldn't wait much longer.

"That wolf," Aurora said once I pulled out a chair for her, "I used to know him. Do you remember that moonflower field we passed through the other day? I used to lie with a pack of rogues in that field. We'd play together and sleep under the stars. They're now trapped in the underworld."

Denise hurried over after grabbing Aurora a glass of water. "Here, take this, sweetie. You're sweating still."

Aurora quickly drank down the glass. "We need to get down there as soon as possible. People are depending on us, our daughter is depending on us, and the entire world is depending on me. And Mars … he's depending on us too."

"Mars?" Denise asked.

Aurora smiled at her. "Mars isn't gone, nor is he with Ares anymore. He's in the underworld."

"How can this be?" Denise asked me with wide eyes. She pushed her glasses up her nose and shook her head, her silver locks falling into her face. "In all my years of practicing, I've never seen or heard anything like this. It's not how it works with DID."

"Would that change if Ares wasn't human?" Aurora asked.

"I guess it could," Denise said, rubbing her wrinkled hands together. "There are significantly less wolves compared to humans and even less wolves with mental illnesses, like DID. I'm assuming things could change … I just didn't think they could be this drastic."

"Ares isn't just a wolf," she said, squeezing my hand.

"We're gods," I said.

"Gods," Denise repeated with a smile. "Well then, there is a lot that we need to talk about, Ares, but I'm so glad that Mars is still out there somewhere. He isn't lost inside of you forever. Would you like Aurora to stay for the remainder of our session?"

I nervously glanced over at her and nodded. "Yes."

I might've hated Denise, but knowing Mars wasn't gone for good made everything a bit better, even with Denise, who loved prying into my head. We would find Mars, keep our pup safe, and save the world.

Talking to her was step one.

CHAPTER 29

ARES

*B*efore the alpha meeting the next morning, I glanced over at Marcel, who now had permanent wrinkles on his forehead from creasing it so much these past few days. Yesterday, Aurora had told me that he would trade his life for Charolette's, and while I so fucking wanted Charolette to live, sacrificing his life was … almost too much to ask.

Even for a coldhearted, hardheaded brute like me.

If Medusa had given us this option weeks ago, I would've fucking forced Marcel to sacrifice his life. But that was the old me. With Mars wandering the underworld and not here, I couldn't make any more stupid and helpless decisions.

He would be disappointed that I had been strong for him but not the rest of this pack.

"You don't have to trade your life for hers," I said to Marcel.

Aurora frowned, tucked some brown hair behind her ear, and placed her hand on my knee. I glanced over at her and smiled, my gaze falling to her belly. I would be strong for her, for me, for this pack, and for our baby.

Never again could I blindly kill people for no good reason at all. I had to survive without my other half and without the man who had *nearly* always talked me down from senseless decisions over the past decade.

"What the fuck are you even saying?" Marcel asked, jerking me out of my thoughts. "I'm surprised you haven't forced me to already."

"I wouldn't do that," I said. "Not anymore. Not without Mars."

At the mention of his alpha's name, Marcel glanced out the window and clenched his sharp jaw. "We have to change with the fucking times, I guess. Do things for the people we love and for the family that we have always known."

"What you're doing is more than I have ever asked of you," I said.

"Well, you didn't ask me to do this," Marcel snapped, his silver hair falling into his face. "I'm doing this because I love your sister. She's my mate, and I would do anything, so she could live and not just survive. She's weakening by the day. I just ..." He trailed off and glared at the rustling trees outside.

"You just what?" Aurora asked softly.

Marcel pressed his trembling lips together. "I wish that I had more time with her. I want to love her for eternity, and now, we only have a couple more days together. It's going to be so fucking hard to leave her. She ... she's never going to forgive me for leaving either."

"You're not going to tell her why you're going?" I asked.

"No," Marcel said, finally turning back to us with that stoic expression painted all over his face. "And I would appreciate it if you didn't either. If she knew ... she would never forgive herself for letting me leave."

* * *

TWENTY MINUTES LATER, alphas from all over the nation piled into the meeting room. I had never seen this many packs represented in one room because shit always started when this many egos decided to talk stuff out.

But this was survival.

If we all wanted to survive, we needed to try.

Elijah stood by the door with his arms crossed over his chest, talking to Adrian. Grabbing Adrian's collar, Elijah yanked him closer, whispered something inaudible into his ear, and then kissed him. Aurora beamed next to me, smacking my shoulder and nodding so obviously toward them.

"They're so cute," she whispered. "So cute!"

When they pulled away, Adrian disappeared down the hallway, and Elijah appeared at Aurora's side. "Who are we still waiting for?"

"Minerva," Aurora said, grinning at Elijah and wiggling her brows.

"You're a creep, Aurora," Elijah teased, adjusting his glasses and sitting. "Anyone else?"

"Medusa too."

Knowing that we didn't have time to waste, I stood and cleared my throat, commanding the attention from every alpha in the room. "While we are waiting for a couple more people, we should strategize. The hounds are becoming more dangerous every day."

"While everyone goes to the underworld, some alphas should stay here," one of the alphas suggested. "There needs to be strong alphas to lead, in case the warriors who travel to the underworld don't come back, similar to how they didn't during the War of the Lycans."

"I agree," Aurora stated. "Some alphas should stay on earth and watch over the men and women and children who aren't traveling to the underworld—at least until we all return. There is no point in leaving if the people on earth aren't safe and protected."

"We need an army down there, Kitten," I said through the mind link. *"Are you sure?"*

She glanced over at me. *"Yes."*

I nodded and sat. "Who will stay?"

The room broke out into a fit of loud murmurs, but then those whispers ceased immediately when Medusa walked into the room, dressed in a seafoam-green gown and veil, and took a seat beside Aurora.

Everyone glanced at her, eyes wide, until someone raised their hand. "I'll stay."

A couple other alphas, who had always taken a negative stance toward war, volunteered to stay on earth too.

And, to my surprise, Vulcan cleared his throat and nodded along with them. "I'll stay to watch over your pack. You both are sacrificing so much for us. I don't want to see it go to waste."

Aurora smiled at him, her eyes glowing gold. "Thank you."

"What about Minerva?" someone asked.

"She'll want to go," I said, balling my hands into fists. "She's stubborn as hell."

Last time I'd tried to force her to stay back, she had run with us all the way to the Syncome Mountains and fought alongside us against the hounds and stone people who attacked so viciously. She wouldn't pass up an opportunity like this.

When the alphas began arranging plans with each other, Aurora turned to Medusa. "Thank you for coming. This means so much to us."

"Of course, sweetheart," Medusa said, setting a hand on her head to still the slithering, restless wolf-like snakes. "Before I forget, has your friend made a decision about Charolette's death? Is he willing to do it?"

I glanced over at Marcel, who stared emptily at the table.

Aurora nodded at Medusa and swallowed hard. "He told me

that he'd do it as long as Charolette never found out about it and only if the cancer will stop while he resides in the underworld and Charolette can live her life out in peace."

Medusa nodded. "It will stop, but Marcel must carry the burden of Hella's wrath."

"He would do anything for Charolette," Aurora whispered, eyes glazing over with tears.

Marcel and Charolette had grown so much over the past couple months. When I'd first brought Aurora back here, they'd hated each other. And now, Marcel was going to sacrifice his life for my sister.

But I could never tell her that.

She would never know that Marcel loved her more than he loved his arrogant self.

"I will talk to him later about it," Aurora said. "He will leave when you need him to."

"Medusa," I started, wrapping an arm around the back of Aurora's seat and leaning forward, "I wanted to ask you something. I don't know if Aurora told you, but I have"—I rolled my eyes—"a thing called dissociative identity disorder—or at least, that's what Denise calls it."

"Yes, I know. You have a personality named Mars too."

"Are you sure you want to talk about this here"—Aurora tensed and glanced at the other alphas—"with everyone?"

After giving her my best smile, I glanced back at Medusa. "During the fight against the hounds, Mars sacrificed himself. Then, a rogue from the underworld—one who told Aurora he had been down there since the War of the Lycans—said that Mars is down there now too. How is that possible?"

I hoped to the fucking gods that Medusa had something because between Denise's knowledge—or lack thereof—and Elijah's science, we were stumped. And it was tearing me up on the inside, almost as much as thinking he was dead.

This shouldn't have been able to happen. Mars didn't live in another body.

Medusa cleared her throat. "When Mars was fatally stabbed, his personality must've separated from your current one. If he's down in the underworld, he isn't a physical being, but perhaps a spirit or a ghostlike entity. Spirits can separate from the body, especially if you're divine, which is how they're able to be reborn. Spirits wander through the depths of the underworld until they are ready and prepared for another body."

"Will he ever be whole again?" Aurora whispered. "If we find him down there, I mean?"

Medusa paused for a long damn time. "When Ares meets Mars, they might or might not form as one again. It depends on a variety of factors, including when both his personalities truly formed within his current body. If his split personality formed when he was reborn into this new body and Ares just stayed dormant until something horrendous happened to Mars, then it's more likely that they'll form into one again. If Ares just appeared later, then it would be more difficult to fuse."

"How will we know?" I asked.

"You won't."

"So, Mars and Ares might be stuck like this forever?" Aurora whispered.

Medusa just gave a curt nod.

"Were Mars and Ares fused together in their past lives?" Aurora asked.

Again, Medusa became quiet. "Yes."

CHAPTER 30

AURORA

*H*ope.

I stared at Ares with a huge grin on my face, my stomach fluttering.

There was a slim chance that Ares and Mars would never become one man again, but they had even been together in their past lives. This could be the sliver of hope that we both so desperately needed.

"Sorry I'm late," Minerva said, shuffling into the room and sitting beside Vulcan.

After throwing Ares another smile, I stood and clapped my hands. Everything was slowly coming together, piece by piece, but it was happening. We had the best shot at destroying the hounds, finding Mars, and raising a pup.

"Now that we're all here," I said, "we may start."

"This is Medusa," Ares said. "She has been alive for thousands of years, even through the War of the Lycans. She has immense knowledge on divine wars. *Don't* act like you know more shit about it than she does because I can assure you that you don't."

Medusa lightly tapped Ares on the shoulder, basically telling him to sit down and not cause any more trouble on her behalf. She never seemed to like the attention anyway. She shifted in the seat next to me, her veil completely covering her face.

"I can help you get to the underworld. I have found a way to get you there, undetected by Hella, the goddess of death, though you will need to trek far to get to her kingdom if we do it this way. One of my acquaintances has been gracious enough to create a map of the underworld for you."

When the alphas burst out into another fit of chatter, Ares cleared his throat. "Let her finish."

"But we need more time," Medusa continued.

"No more waiting," I declared, cradling my bump. "We need to get there as soon as possible. We don't have much time left, and I don't want the hounds coming to earth to slaughter innocent packs."

Medusa turned her head in my direction, the snakes under her veil slithering around crazily. "We cannot rush this, Aurora. It's what your brother did, and look where it got him—stuck in the underworld for hundreds of years."

"I'm done thinking this through." I pulled the bottom of my shirt up to show her the scar I'd gotten last night, which ran across my stomach. It was closed but still raw and rough against my soft skin. "Nyx has threatened my family."

"Nyx," Medusa whispered, placing a hand on my belly. Though she didn't remove her veil, by the crack in her voice, I could tell that she was on the verge of tears over Nyx trying to hurt me. She glided her fingers against my bare skin and traced the scar on my stomach. "How did she do this?"

"Through a memory," I said. "Can she do that?"

"If you were in a dreamlike state, then yes." Medusa nodded.

"Appearing in dreams and affecting people in real life is one of her strongest powers, though it does take a lot of energy out of her to do so. What did you see in that memory?"

I gulped, not wanting to relive it, but knowing that I had to, for the sake of everyone. "Nyx killed me and blamed it on her love for Helios. I had seen the memory before, but this time, we ended up in a dark room. She was older and was trying to kill my baby."

Medusa blew a breath out through her nose. "Somewhat similar to the way that you and Ares are mates, Helios and Nyx are mates. Helios rejected her after he found out that she killed you in a past life, and Nyx trapped him down in the underworld. If he comes to earth, so do the other underworld gods. They are tied together by a divine bond. Helios can't leave until it's broken."

Then, it was settled. We needed to go. Now.

"We need to stop the war, free the gods who have been tied to the underworld, and release the rogues from Hella's cruel powers. Some of those hounds down there are not undead, but wolves that had been taken down to the underworld during the War of the Lycans."

Yet, while I spoke, Medusa was still stuck on the fact that Nyx had appeared to me. She tapped a finger against her chin and shook her head from side to side. "If Nyx appeared to you, that means that she knows about your baby now, and it's even more important that you do as I said as soon as you give birth—that way, they cannot find out who your baby is."

"What'd she say?" Ares asked me.

"You didn't tell Ares about what we discussed?" Medusa asked.

I glanced over at Ares, nervously gnawing on the inside of my lip. Though I hadn't wanted to tell him because of how hurt he'd acted these past few days, I didn't want him to hurt now or feel like I'd purposely hidden something so huge from him.

Honestly, I had *kinda* talked to him about it.

"What didn't you tell me?" Ares asked, brows furrowed.

"We already talked about it. Medusa told me to give away the baby," I said through clenched teeth.

I squeezed his hand tighter and tried hard not to let my emotions get to me, but after years of being treated like shit and crying myself to sleep, I wanted some damn happiness in my life. This baby was that joy.

So, I shook my head. "I told her no."

"This should be an easy decision for you," Medusa said. "Think of the child."

"You expect me to give up my baby like it's nothing?!" I said, shaking my head and vowing to myself that I would not cry anymore. After everything that had happened these past few days, I knew giving our girl away would be the right thing to do, especially to keep her safe, but I didn't want to just leave her.

Between Dad and Mom and my old packmates, I'd never really had anyone. Our girl would be the one person who I could love truly. I wanted to give her a life that I'd never had, and I wanted her to experience life with a mother and father who loved her more than life itself.

Medusa tilted her head in my direction. "I don't expect you to give up your baby and not feel bad about it. I expect you to make the hard decision to give your baby a better life than the one you're in now. I had to do it with you."

"What?" I whispered, eyes wide. "What did you say?"

Medusa gulped, turned away from the alphas, and pulled the seafoam-green veil over her face, the snakes on her head suddenly stilling. Medusa grabbed my hand and squeezed it tightly in hers, the warmth from them spreading throughout my entire body. "I had to give you up, so you could grow up in an environment that was safe and where you could get stronger."

No.

It couldn't be.

"You're …" I started. "You're my …"

"Your mother," Medusa said. "I'm your real mother."

CHAPTER 31

AURORA

*W*as Medusa my real mother?

No, she can't be.

Since birth, Mom had raised me alongside Jeremy as if we were siblings. She never mentioned once that I had been adopted or that I was never really her child. But if this was true, all the name-calling, all the rude remarks, everything about the way she'd treated me would make sense.

In some unfortunate way.

Yet in every myth and legend that I had learned in school, Medusa couldn't get pregnant. After the decline of the gods, she had been cursed for eternity to never be able to conceive a child and especially not to survive the birth of one. If this was real, was that myth false?

"You're not lying," I whispered to her, brows furrowed. "Are you?"

"No," she said, taking my face in her hands. "You're my daughter. Venus, goddess of fertility, blessed me with a child after I tried and failed to conceive one for thousands upon thousands of years." Medusa stared at me with eyes so teary that they looked bloodshot. "And I had to give that child up, so she could have a better life."

My lips trembled, throat drying. With my spine being fucked, the hounds always after me, and my pack putting me down, my life had been decent at best. It hadn't been the worst life I could've been granted, but maybe it would've been better with Medusa. I would never know.

"Why? Why did you give me up?" I whispered, unable to form any other words.

The reason was clear—Hella and Nyx wanted me to stay dead. But I didn't want to believe that my own mother would let me endure life with this fucking disability and with that dreadful woman who had always put me down behind my back.

If I had been with Medusa since birth, I might've been able to grow and become stronger, and I might not have had to deal with the threat of relentless hounds. I would've been able to lead a somewhat-normal life without the back problems and without the constant criticism.

"I was never supposed to have children, and I was never supposed to be immortal. It was wished by so many gods and goddesses that I die, that I never bore children to bring into this world. They said that they would be as ugly as me, would turn people to stone with the lift of a finger, and would possess properties that were stronger than all other gods combined. You were never supposed to happen," Medusa whispered as she stroked her fingers over my cheeks. "But I'm so glad you did. I have watched you grow up from afar and become such a strong warrior, which I knew your old pack would make you."

"No," I snapped, wanting her to know how fucked up she had made me. "My pack hated me!"

Medusa tucked some hair behind my ear, lips trembling. "They made you strong. That's what I needed your mother to do because you won't be able to defeat the gods of the underworld with love and kindness. They will betray you and hurt you, Aurora. They are out to kill you again."

Overcome with anger, I pressed my lips together, my chest tightening. "Did you tell my mother to hate me? Did you tell her that I deserved to be talked about behind my back? Is that how you think I got strong?"

Medusa went to hug me, but I held my hand up to keep her back.

"I became detached by watching my brother die and then killing him again. I became strong by learning to fight when I was broken after the hounds nearly slaughtered me. I became powerful with the Malavite Stone. It had nothing to do with that woman you gave your child to."

Ares wrapped his arm around my shoulders and pulled me closer. "Kitten, calm down." He rubbed small, soothing circles on my shoulders. "Take a deep breath for me. Your heart is pounding so loudly that I can hear it."

Knowing that I could be endangering the baby, I took a deep breath like Ares had instructed and placed a hand on my belly to feel my baby kick. Medusa was telling me this because she wanted me to be comfortable with giving my baby away, but I hated finding out this way.

"Were you ever going to tell me that I was your child?" I asked when I calmed down.

Medusa gazed at me for a few moments and then looked down at her lap. "No. I wanted you to love that woman despite everything she did to you. She'd selflessly taken you in when I asked her to raise you, and she raised an alpha who is strong enough to defeat the gods."

"And my father?" I asked. "Who is he?"

"You don't have one." she said. "I hadn't been with another man or god for thousands of years, and I found myself pregnant with you. From the moment I found out, I knew that you weren't just anyone who possessed the powers of a god, but you were Dawn, the goddess. If Hella or Nyx had found out that I was raising a child without a father, they'd have known it was you. I had to give you away to keep you safe."

A deafening silence erupted over the entire room, no alpha daring to say a word. I sat back in my seat, pushed my head into my hands, and cried hard, my body shaking. Whatever I had been holding in these past few weeks—whether it was finding Ares cutting himself or trying to be strong for this pack or watching wolf after wolf die from the hounds—I let it all out.

Medusa was my mother.

My true mother.

And she had given me up to protect me from the gods' wrath.

I wrapped my arms around my knees and pulled them to my chest. How could she have let me endure all those years of pain with my mother—or whoever she was? Didn't she know how much I hated it there? Had she checked up on me or made sure that I was okay or ever fucking regretted her decision of giving me away?

"Do you regret it?" I whispered, pushing some tears away. "Do you regret not getting to see me or raise me or watch me grow up? Do you regret that I always looked up to that woman as my mother and had love for her at one point because she was my family? Do you regret any of it?"

Medusa looked me right in the eye and said, "No," with so much certainty. "I don't regret it, and neither will you. But, Aurora, you will regret it if anything happens to your child. You will hate yourself for putting her in harm's way. Don't put her in Hella's path. Don't let her die because you're being selfish and only thinking about how this will affect you. You need the child, but if she dies, you won't have her."

While I wanted to hate Medusa for everything that she was, I couldn't deny her words. If anything happened to my baby because I'd brought her to the underworld or I hadn't given her away, then I would regret it for the rest of my life.

Deciding that I couldn't speak another word to her, I pressed my lips together and sank in my chair, tears still pouring down my cheeks. Medusa, my own mother, didn't regret giving me away. The woman who had raised me loathed me.

Who the fuck loved me besides Ares and Jeremy?

Nobody.

I had no fucking family.

Across the table, Vulcan cleared his throat and leaned forward in his seat. "I don't mean to interrupt, but did you say Venus granted you a child?"

Medusa pulled her veil over her face to shield her eyes from the other mortal alphas and nodded at him. "Yes, Vulcan, the goddess Venus granted me Aurora."

A wave of emotion crossed his face—sadness, grief, sorrow, and finally happiness. "If it's the same woman, she … she is—was my mate. The last time I saw her was in the field of the stone people. She had left me years ago, turned to stone, and never came home to me."

Medusa tensed. "Yes, she is the same woman you speak of."

"Is she alive?"

"Venus is alive and in the underworld with Helios to try to stop this war."

"My Venus is … is a goddess," Vulcan whispered, lips curling into a smile.

Though I wanted to be happy for him and though I tried my best to smile, I couldn't get myself to do it. Another person was trapped in the underworld, trying to stop this war before it spilled out onto the soil and destroyed all life forever.

"Yes," Medusa said. "She is the goddess of fertility, who never typically sets foot in a war zone. Yet these past few hundred years have changed her. Since the gods aren't worshipped as much anymore, they have lost much of their powers and have had to do things that they normally wouldn't do to keep earth safe."

Vulcan nearly doubled over the table. "Why? Why would she leave for the underworld and leave me here? Why didn't she take me with her? I would've fought for her. We could've had pups. Will she ever come back?"

Medusa placed her hand on his and squeezed it gently. "Though she is the goddess of fertility, Venus has lost her own fertility due to the lack of worship. She found out she could not have children just after she met you. She didn't want to disappoint you, so she departed from this world and decided to fight to keep you safe."

As I listened to them speak, my chest tightened. Nothing seemed worse than not being able to conceive a child, especially when she was part of a pack. It was almost a given that mates bore pups almost immediately after they mated. Every pack loved the children and treated them as if they were their own.

Not being able to have pups was devastating.

"It's actually quite terrible," Medusa continued. "She would've made such a great mother, always warm and caring. She loves children whether they're hers or not; she would do anything for them. These past few years have been the hardest on her."

Ares tugged me into a hug and placed his lips on my temple. "And who else knows about her inability to have children?" Ares asked, body tense and rigid against mine. He rubbed more soothing circles around my shoulder and leaned closer to me, slipping his hand around my stomach to gently grasp my baby bump.

"I was the only one with her when she found out. She is ashamed of it."

"This doesn't leave this room," Vulcan said, possessiveness in every one of his words.

"It can't," Medusa said. "Not only for Venus's sake, but also for the sake of all the wolves about to enter the underworld. Nobody can know this potential weakness that we have on our side. Nyx will use it to make Venus go insane and turn on you all."

After blowing out a deep breath, I rested my head on Ares's shoulder and pushed away my tears with the backs of my hands. Ares hugged me close and gently stroked my stomach, his fingers against it.

Our baby kicked, and I hated—fucking loathed—the thought of giving her away.

How could I do it? And who did I trust to take care of her?

It had to be someone that Hella and Nyx didn't know about already, which meant that Elijah was out of the picture. I had grown up with him, and surely, they would find that out. They would torture him first to find her.

"I know that you don't want to do this, Kitten," Ares whispered into my ear, "and I understand why. You don't want to lose someone else who means the world to you. You watched your brother die twice, you watched Mars leave, and now, our baby is in danger."

I curled into his chest and whimpered in response.

"If we go to the underworld with our daughter, she will be in danger too," Ares reasoned.

"Can you imagine a life without our daughter?" I asked him, wanting an honest answer. "Can you imagine not seeing your daughter for almost twenty years, like Medusa didn't see me? Can you imagine not getting to watch her grow, play with other pups, and do everything we dreamed of her doing?"

"I would rather her have a good life here with some other family than a terrible one in the unruly underworld, where her life will always be threatened," he said with tears in his eyes. "I hate saying it out loud, but it's true."

More tears streamed down my face. He had been looking forward to having a child for so damn long. I didn't want him to just give up on her. But … this was for the best, no matter how fucking bad it hurt.

"Who will take care of her?" I asked. "It can't be Elijah."

Ares glanced over at Vulcan. "Maybe Venus and Vulcan. We'll just have to get her out of the underworld."

CHAPTER 32

ARES

*M*y dark, raging heart ticked violently.

Giving up our pup made me want to detonate and destroy.

And while the old Ares would run into war, into battle, or into a mere conversation, thinking that his plans were the greatest, now, I forced myself to step back and really think about my daughter.

We needed to give her up for as long as it took to keep her safe.

Part of me thought that this was my way to avoid being a bad father, but deep down, I knew that I was doing this for Aurora and the well-being of our baby. Aurora wouldn't let me go down to the underworld alone, and because of that, we needed our baby to be safe.

"Will Venus come back to earth to spend the rest of her life with Vulcan when we go down to the underworld?" Aurora asked

Medusa, her voice trembling. When she curled her fingers around mine on her stomach, the baby kicked again.

Medusa turned toward us. "Possibly. She is currently my point of contact and already knows about you coming down there to defeat the gods of the underworld. She knows the plan and knows people who can help you out. She is tired of fighting though. This isn't her forte, so she might accept returning to earth."

"That's what we'll do then," I declared.

"Let's take a break and regroup in an hour to come up with a solid plan," Aurora said.

Once the alphas stood and headed out, Elijah and Vulcan lingered behind. Just before the door could shut to leave us to speak in peace, Ruffles sauntered into the room with Pringle trailing behind her. Her stomach nearly grazed against the ground, and she brushed up against my leg.

"Damn, Ruffles, you're about to pop," I said, sitting her in my lap and stroking her fur.

Cats had a shorter pregnancy than wolves, but … I hadn't thought it was *this* much shorter. It was almost as short as Aurora's.

Pringle had Ruffles's blue hat pinned between his sharp teeth. After he nudged Aurora, Aurora picked it up and placed it on Ruffles's head, scratching her chin when she purred so loudly that everyone in the entire room heard it.

"We need to talk to you, Vulcan," I said.

Vulcan sat across from us and nodded. "Anything."

"If we get Venus to come home …" I started.

I glanced over at Aurora to make sure that this was okay. I would do anything to keep my girls safe and happy and secure. Eyes wavering with tears, Aurora frowned and nodded to me, as if to tell me that it was okay to give our only child away.

"We need you to take our daughter in, Vulcan."

Vulcan glanced down at Aurora's stomach with wide eyes.

Tears streamed down her cheeks, yet she nodded again and pleaded with him through her sadness, "Please, Vulcan, you have to do this for us. We can't bring her."

"A baby—*your* baby—is a lot of responsibility," Vulcan said quietly, his voice tight and his lips pressed together. "She's going to be beyond strong and powerful. But I'll ... I'll make her stronger. I'll protect her for you."

Aurora clutched onto my arm, her pain so unbearable that even I could feel her heart breaking. The last thing I wanted was to give our baby away, but if we ever wanted her to have a normal sort of life, we had to do this.

Medusa sat beside Aurora and placed her hand on her thigh. "It's okay, sweetie. Everything is going to be okay. I give my word that I'll be up here to protect her for as long as she lives."

"For as long as you live," Aurora corrected.

"For as long as I live," Medusa repeated, setting her hand upon Aurora's. "She'll be the most powerful wolf this world has ever known."

Glancing between them, I pursed my lips and cleared my throat to command everyone's attention. "I need to have a moment alone with Aurora. Come back in twenty minutes, and we'll resume the meeting."

Aurora wasn't and would never be okay with this. Neither would I.

But pain plagued every part of her body from the inside out right now, and I needed to make her feel better. She was the love of my life, my mate for eternity, and the mother of my child. Mars might be gone, but she stayed by my side still.

She didn't make me feel worse about his disappearance.

And I would support her through anything.

Once the room cleared, I shut the door and turned on my heel toward Aurora. Before I could stop her, she shoved me against the wall and pressed her hungry lips against mine, her entire body trembling in pain.

"Aurora," I managed to say between kisses, "are you okay?"

"I don't want to talk, Ares," she said, a tear slipping down her cheek. "I want to forget." She balled my shirt in her hands and yanked me closer. "Forget about how I'm agreeing to something I swore I'd never do."

The last time she'd wanted to forget with sex was after she killed Jeremy.

Though I was successfully able to stop her and hold her, something told me that this time, she wouldn't give in. She really, truly wanted to forget about this for a couple moments. And so did I.

So, I grasped her hips and pushed her pants to her ankles, taking her in my arms and setting her down on the chair I'd sat in during the meeting. She laced a hand into my hair and tossed her head back, more tears flowing down her cheeks.

"Please, help me forget."

Pain shooting through my chest, I knelt in front of my mate, spread her legs, and buried my face between her thighs, my tongue flicking out against her clit. She arched her back, the sobs escaping her lips, and pulled my face closer to her cunt.

"More," she pleaded. "Please, more."

I held her hips down and steady against the chair, my tongue flicking out faster and harder, the more she squirmed under me. Her legs began to shake in my hands, and she squeezed her eyes closed and pressed a hand to her mouth to muffle her sobs.

"Open your eyes, Aurora," I growled against her aching cunt. "If you want to forget, look at *me*. Watch *me*. Don't shield your eyes. Don't stare into the darkness." I stuck a finger into her pussy, hating that I was doing this to help her forget, but knowing it was the only way to ease the pain. "Come on me."

She opened her eyes and stared down at me through watery

orbs. Tears poured down her cheeks, but I reached up and pushed each one of them away as my tongue flicked and rolled around her clit.

When I sucked it into my mouth, a soft moan escaped her mouth.

"Oh Goddess," she moaned, gripping my hair and grinding her pussy against my face to pleasure herself. "Ares, I ..." She bucked her hips. "Please, I ... more. Ares, I need more from you. Make me forget."

I pulled my face away from her pussy, picked her up, and sat in her spot. Once I pushed my jeans to my knees, I rested her back on top of me with her trembling legs on either side of mine. When she settled down, I lifted my hips enough to meet hers and slid into my mate.

She wrapped her arms around my shoulders and kissed me hard on the mouth, moving her hips up and down. "I'm sorry. I'm so sorry that they're after me. I'm sorry that we have to give up our baby because of me."

Slowing my pace until I stopped completely, I grasped her jaw in my hand and looked her in the eyes. "This is not your fault. You've done everything in your power to protect our daughter. We will come back, and we will see her again. Don't blame yourself."

Another sob escaped her lips, and I pulled out of her. This wasn't what I wanted, nor was it what she needed right now, no matter how much she tried to convince me otherwise. Instead, I wrapped her up into my arms and let her cry her big heart out into my chest.

"I love her so much already," she whimpered. "I can't believe that I'm agreeing to this."

"Me neither," I said, gently stroking her hair. "But we need to, for her sake." I gathered her face in my hands once more and placed my lips on hers. "If we don't do this, she might die in the hands of Hella and Nyx. I don't want that to happen, and neither do you."

"I know," she said, voice barely above a whisper. "It's just hard."

"Life is really hard, Aurora." I shook my head and glanced down at my wrists. "Really hard sometimes."

CHAPTER 33

AURORA

"Say good-bye to your loved ones, make arrangements with your packs, and meet back here in five days. We will go to the underworld to end this all," I said to the alphas at the end of our meeting.

In the hours we had met, everyone had agreed upon who would travel to the underworld, which warriors from which packs were needed, and how we were going to get there without being seen or heard.

It had been way more productive than our last few meetings, especially with this many alphas here.

After everyone bowed their heads in response and agreement, alphas piled out of the room and flooded out of the meeting house, heading back home. When all the alphas and warriors were gone, Medusa glanced over at Vulcan and placed her hand on his shoulder.

"If we hurry, we can chat with Venus today. All we have to do is get back to Stone Valley. She is typically active on earth during early dusk, awaiting my conversation. Tonight, specifically, we planned to meet, so I could speak to her about getting you all to the underworld."

Vulcan suddenly froze, the blood draining from his cheeks. "All this time ..." he whispered, tears filling the brim of his eyes. "All this time, I could've seen her. I can't believe that she wanted to spend eternity away from me. If I go with you, will she even want to see me?"

My chest tightened, a frown stretching across my lips. Vulcan had spent years thinking that he had lost his mate and would never get a chance to speak with her again. Now, when faced with the information that she had left him and had the ability to come back to earth, he was both devastated and ... unsure of everything.

If I were him, I would be too.

"I want to go," Vulcan clarified, brows furrowing. "But not if she doesn't want to see me."

Medusa ushered him to the door, her seafoam-green tunic swaying behind her and her snakes actively slithering around on her head. "My dear, she has never stopped talking about you. Every time I see her, she always asks me to check up on you and asks how you are. She'll be grateful to see you again."

When we walked out of the building, a chilling fall breeze blew my hair in hundreds of directions, similar to the way the snakes moved on Medusa's head when she let them break free of her veil. I pulled my hair back into a ponytail and glanced up at Ares.

"Does this mean we're running?" I asked, cradling my bump.

Though I could shift with ease now, my baby made running harder by the day. Longer runs especially had become increasingly hard this past week. I had needed to slow down multiple times the last time I trained.

Ares ran a hand across my belly. "You can stay here."

"No. I'm coming with you." I wrapped my hand around his

and hurried after Medusa, who walked farther into the woods. "But I need you to run with me, Ares. It's more difficult than before."

Ruffles and Pringle followed us to the edge of the clearing and watched us curiously.

"*Meow!*"

Ares glanced over at Ruffles, who rubbed up against him and purred louder than she usually did. Pringle sashayed over and sniffed her butt. Ruffles meowed again and turned around to swat him in the head. Pringle took her hit and walked closer to her, licking her neck.

After crouching down, Ares scratched Ruffles's head and told her we'd be back soon. To my surprise, Ruffles brushed against me and purred even louder than I had ever heard her before, the sound almost amplified somehow.

She was more sociable than usual today.

I grabbed Ares's hand, walked farther out into the forest to be alone with him, and crouched on all fours. Beckoning my beast, I transformed into a pregnant she-wolf with my belly swollen and inches off the ground.

When we approached, Vulcan stood next to Medusa, ready to run. On our way to the field of stone, my paws hit the ground as we ran ahead through the desolate Hound Territory lands. Usually, hounds crawled through this forest, searching for prey, but tonight, the woods were particularly silent.

Ares nudged my hind leg. "*You're doing good, Kitten.*"

Pushing myself a bit harder, I continued through the forest, careful not to scrape my belly against the ground and disrupt my growing child. Even with my caution, we made it to the field, almost in record time. We slowed to a stop in front of the mile-long field of stone people.

But this time, the field was nearly empty.

Most of the inhabitants had fought and turned into stone back at Ares's former property, though still, some stragglers, like

Venus, stood tall and proud here. I shifted into my human form and walked naked through the broken rocks.

Dressed in silks that swayed in the wind and with a stoic yet soft expression on her face, Venus stood among the chaos of fallen and fighting gods, wolves, and hounds. As I approached Venus, Vulcan shifted beside me and ran a hand through his thick dark-red scruff to make himself look presentable, and then he paced beside me.

"I'm so nervous," he said. "I haven't seen her in years."

"Gods and goddesses, you run faster than I thought," Medusa said, jogging toward us and bending at the hip with her hands on her knees. She handed us some clothes from her home and placed her hand on her chest to catch her breath.

After making a full recovery, Medusa stepped in front of Venus and pulled back her veil.

At first, Venus didn't move.

Then, her eyes shifted from side to side until they landed on Vulcan.

Suddenly, she came alive, the stone breaking off her and crumbling to the ground.

Vulcan and Venus stared at each other for a few long moments, both their eyes wavering. Venus blinked a few times, opening and closing her mouth, and finally succumbed to the tears.

"Vulcan," she said, voice barely over a whisper, "I can't believe you're here."

I intertwined my fingers with Ares's and squeezed his hand. While I wanted to smile, I couldn't because all I could see was the love and pain and heartbreak in their eyes. Leaving the man she loved on earth to dive into the underworld for years must've hurt worse than anything.

And soon, that would be me with my baby.

I didn't know how we would be able to pack up and leave everyone we cared about—Ares's father, Charolette, Elijah, and our daughter. It was more than either of us had bargained for, but this was for more than just us.

This was a divine war.

Finally, Vulcan scooped Venus up in his arms and spun her around in the air, stuffing his face into her neck, like Ares always did with me. Venus grinned, her ivory hair swaying in the breeze, and wrapped her arms around his shoulders until her fingers turned white.

"I'm so sorry for leaving you," she said when he placed her down. Stroking his jaw with her fingers, she touched him in awe, as if she still couldn't believe how he was reacting to her. She must've expected him to hate her for leaving.

Vulcan shook his head and pushed a tear away with the back of his hand. "It's okay." He rested his forehead against hers. "Don't apologize to me about that. You should've told me that you couldn't ... you couldn't have children. I would've understood."

Venus placed a hand over her mouth and sobbed. "You were so elated about having pups. I didn't have the heart to break it to you. And"—she glanced around until her eyes landed on me—"I wanted to protect everyone until Dawn and Ares were reborn."

After pulling away from Vulcan, Venus threw her arms around us. "I can't believe I'm seeing you both again. You look the same, the exact same, even after the transition from one body to another."

I ran a hand over my belly bump and frowned at her. "Your time in the underworld is over, Venus. You need to rest. It's taken so much out of you, hasn't it?"

"I can't," she said, glancing down at my stomach and straightening her shoulders. "You're pregnant. You cannot go down there. Those beasts will trap you there and won't let you leave. There are far too many rogues from earth that you'll want to save. And, plus, you're the goddess that they're trying to slaughter for the rest of eternity."

Refusing to back down, I held eye contact with her. "That's

why I'm going. If they want me, then I'll be sure to give them a fair fight. I don't know shit about the underworld, but I will defeat them this time—for my daughter."

Venus shook her head. "And what will happen when your daughter is born?"

Medusa placed a hand on Venus's shoulder. "You will take care of her until Aurora and Ares come back to earth."

Venus stared at Medusa with wide eyes. "But they'll be trap—"

Medusa shushed Venus. "Aurora has already made her choice. She won't back down. I have begged her to. You and Vulcan will raise their baby until they come back. It doesn't matter how long it takes. They are both warriors and will come home alive."

My stomach twisted into knots. *Would we?*

After grimacing, Venus slumped her shoulders forward and let the stress of the underworld tumble off her. "Okay," she whispered, tucking some ivory hair behind her ear. "I'll stay up here and watch her with Vulcan, but you have to promise that you'll come back. Your daughter needs her parents."

"We promise," Ares said. "We'll come back for her."

CHAPTER 34

ARES

*W*hen we arrived back home, Pringle scurried from the kitchen into a back room with a bag of Ruffles Chips between his teeth. I arched my brow at him and concluded that Ruffles had meowed at him until he brought back her favorite food.

I curled my arm around Aurora and glanced into the kitchen at Marcel.

He sat at the table with a glass of rum in one hand, staring emptily down, silver hair covering his face. "I'm going to fucking miss her."

Aurora stopped and frowned at him, squeezing my hand. "Me too," she whispered.

Marcel grabbed the glass so hard that it shattered in his hand, blood dripping onto the table from his palm. "How the hell am I going to fucking live without my mate? How can I never see her again? She's going to fucking loathe every part of me."

"You're going to figure out a way because she's your mate." I glanced over at Aurora and thought back to why Mars had sacrificed himself for her without a second thought. "We would do anything for the person we love even if they didn't think it was the right thing."

Grumbling to himself, Marcel grabbed the bottle of rum and put it to his lips. "I want to be alone."

After taking one last glance at Marcel, I guided Aurora up the stairs to our bedroom with one of my hands around her hip and the other around the railing. Aurora moved slowly up the stairs, cradling her belly and frowning.

"How are you feeling, Kitten?" I asked. "How's your back after the run?"

"It was fine, but I don't know how much more I'll be able to run before she's born."

When we reached the top of the stairs, I wrapped both arms around her from behind and pulled her to my chest, burying my face into the crook of her neck. "Bed rest," I said, kissing my mark. "I'll make sure that you don't move from our bed for the rest of this week."

She giggled, the sound drifting through the pack house. "Ares, I don't think—"

Before she could finish, I gently pressed her against the hallway wall. "Oh, Kitten, don't worry. It won't be hard to keep you there." I trailed my nose up the column of her neck. "We can start now, if you're *that* excited about it." I slipped a hand between her legs. "Spread your legs for me."

This would probably be our last time together for a while.

And I wanted to make sure Aurora knew just how much I appreciated her.

"But Marcel ..." Aurora said.

"Marcel is leaving the house," I said loud enough for Marcel to hear. "Isn't he?"

"I'll be at the Pink Moon Tavern if you need me!" Marcel shouted up the stairs.

When the front door closed, I growled in Aurora's ear, "Now, spread your legs."

Once she inched her feet apart and arched her back, I slipped her pants down to her knees and slid three fingers up into her, thrusting them slowly at first. She moaned softly and clenched on me so tightly that I couldn't stop imagining my dick inside her.

"I'll be gentle with you, Kitten." I ground my hips against hers, rubbing my wet fingers against her clit. Laying hot, wet kisses up her neck, I captured her earlobe between my teeth and grunted low in her ear.

"I want you inside of me," she whispered. "Please ..."

"Fuck," I mumbled against her neck. After pulling out my cock, I pressed the head right against her entrance and placed a hand around the front of her stomach for support, and then I slipped myself inside of her, giving her an inch at a time.

When I was deep inside her pussy, she clenched around me and dug her nails into the wall, her choppy breaths filling the hallway. With every thrust, I found myself coming closer and closer to the edge already.

My mate's cunt was too slippery and too tight for me to last much longer.

"Harder, Alpha ..." she said.

Canines brushing against her shoulder, I bit down tenderly. "Those soft, little, desperate moans are such a tease, Kitten."

"More," she whispered. "Give me more."

I spit on my fingers, rubbed them against her clit, and started to pump myself faster inside of her, my thrusts long and slow, hitting her G-spot every single time. She bit her lip to suppress another moan.

"Is this what you want?" I asked, wrapping my hand around the front of her throat.

"Yes," she said, breathy.

"Your pussy just got so tight for me," I grunted.

Fuck.

This woman was going to make me come so fucking hard for her.

"Yes," she said. "I love it."

I wrapped my hand in her hair and pulled her toward me, so her back was arched. After growling low, I thrust hard up into her pussy while my fingers brushed against her clit. Her pussy quivered on me, and she cried out.

I was unable to stop myself as pleasure rushed out of my dick and into her pussy. She clenched on me even harder, her pussy sucking the cum right out. I slowly pulled out of her and groaned into her ear. She took a deep breath through her nose and relaxed against the wall.

The cum slowly dripped down her inner thighs from her creamed pussy. I picked her up and brought her to our bedroom, setting her on the bed and grabbing a towel from the bathroom. I wiped the cum from her thighs and her pussy lips, cleaning her up.

Just as I finished, Ruffles shrieked in the other room.

Aurora placed a hand on her lower back to stabilize herself and stood up, waddling to the door. "What is going on with her? She sounds like she's dying, for goodness' sake."

Ruffles shrieked again.

I grasped Aurora's hand and guided her to a spare bedroom. Inside, Ruffles lay on her side in pain as Pringle stood beside her and licked her head. Aurora's eyes widened. Red discharge covered the sheets. Aurora stepped back and grasped my bicep, pulling me back with her.

"She's giving birth," she whispered to me with a proud-mom smile on her face. "My Ruffles is giving birth."

CHAPTER 35

AURORA

*R*uffles lay Frito and Funyun—her two gray kittens—on my lap and then cuddled up next to me on the suede couch, letting Cheeto, the Siamese cat, and Dorito, the mix of gray and Siamese, lie on her tummy. With her blue hat on, Ruffles smiled up at me and purred.

It was the night before the alphas and their packs would descend into the underworld, and my stomach was swollen beyond belief. I had hoped all week that our baby would be ready to come into this world, but she had stayed away for as long as she could.

Maybe that was for the better.

Overcome with sadness that we'd have to leave soon, I stroked Ruffles's fur and slumped against the couch, listening to Venus talk about the underworld and give Ares, Marcel, and me some tips about what to do when we got there.

"The first time you arrive in the underworld—and the first time only—you will need to cross the Acheron River by the passage of Charon's ferry. Though he is undead, like many of the hounds, he is in no relation to Hella and rarely speaks to anyone who is divine. It should be safe for you to cross without problem and without Hella's knowledge."

After licking Cheeto on the head, Ruffles turned toward Venus. "*Meow.*"

I nodded at Ruffles in agreement and rested a hand on my bump. "Yes, after we cross the river, what do we do then? I've heard that there are multiple kingdoms in the underworld. Where is Nyx and Hella's kingdom located? Do we have to go through other kingdoms to get there? How will we know where to go?"

Venus sat up straight and crossed one leg over the other, her lovely, silky locks flowing down her back. The moonlight flooded into the room through the window and illuminated her olive skin, making me a bit jealous. How could one be so innately beautiful?

"First," Venus started, curling her fingers around strands of her thick hair, "you will meet with Cerberus, the three-headed hellhound, who will let you officially enter into the underworld. Again, Cerberus is under Hades's control and does not typically associate with Hella or Nyx."

Vulcan grasped her shoulder and rubbed gently. "Is Cerberus a threat?"

"A threat?" Venus laughed. "No, Cerberus will not be a threat to you. He's intimidating at first with three heads and foaming at all mouths, but … he won't actually hurt divine beings. He'll bark and roar, but Hades won't let him attack any divines entering the underworld unless they provoke him first."

Frito weakly stood on all four legs and curled closer to Funyun in my lap.

"Then, where?" I asked, gently stroking their fur.

Venus blew out a deep breath, her shoulders slumping forward. "From there, I would suggest that you meet with Hades.

He doesn't get involved in divine politics, but he will provide you with a map and some tips to navigate the underworld. He might seem like an annoyed man at first, but he's just been trapped down in the underworld with nobody for way too long."

"Seems like he needs a woman," Marcel said, kicking back on the couch next to Ruffles and locking his hands behind his head, biceps flexing. He eyed Venus and raised a brow. "From the myths we learned in school, he might need more than that."

Venus shushed him. "Oh, stop it. Those myths are nothing like the real gods. We're more than our stories. Myths made Hades out to be the bad guy, but once you get to know him, he's actually a sweetheart, just deeply misunderstood."

Vulcan growled possessively, his grip tightening just a bit on Venus's shoulder.

Venus brushed him off and pushed him away slightly. "Don't be jealous. I'm sure you've slept with other people since I was gone too."

Another warning growl exited Vulcan's throat, but Venus didn't even look fazed. In fact, she looked amused more than anything with a sly smile and sparkling eyes. She waved a dismissive hand. "Anyway"—she looked over at Marcel—"while everyone should go directly to Hades, you, Marcel, should go to Tartarus, where you'll find Hella and ask for a life trade."

Marcel sat up straight, body tense, and nodded toward the open door. Ares looked out of it to make sure Charolette wasn't listening in on our meeting and shut the door, so Venus's voice wouldn't travel and echo in Mom's grand pack house.

"Do not associate yourself with Aurora, Ares, or any of the other alphas coming into the underworld," Venus continued. "That means no hugging, no good-byes, no scent lingering on your clothes. If Hella or Nyx captures even the smallest scent of them on you or finds you dreaming of them, they will kill you. Then, your mate will die."

Marcel rubbed a hand across his face. "I've lived with them

for over twenty-seven years now," Marcel said, shaking his head of silver hair. "How am I supposed to get rid of their scent and the thought of them?"

Venus cleared her throat. "Twenty miles from the arrival zone, in the Acheron River, there is a pool that you will bathe in. It will burn your clothes and the top layer of your skin, giving you a fresh scent, almost as if you were reborn."

"Burn his skin?" Ares asked, brows furrowed. "All the way off?"

"It's a painful process, but you'll get through it." She glanced at me. "Aurora did as a baby after Medusa had to give her up. Medusa couldn't leave any scent or trace of her on Aurora or else Hella and Nyx would have found her."

I swallowed hard and frowned. This past month, I had been so rude to Medusa because she'd suggested that I give up my baby, but I hadn't realized that she had given up so much when she did the same with me.

"And then?" I said, shame spreading through my body. "Then, what do we do?"

"After visiting Hades, you will start your trek to Tartarus," Venus said, placing a map in my hand and wrapping my fingers around it. "This will help you. It was the best I could do with the terrain that I'd traveled through, but either way, you must be prepared. It has been hundreds of years since I've been to some of these places. The terrain might've changed, and you will fight monster after monster to get there."

Grasping the fragile map, I glanced from Marcel to Ares. "We're going to do this. We're going to save our world."

CHAPTER 36

ARES

Aurora lay beside me in the bed, her soft snores drifting through my ears. I stared up at the ceiling and breathed steadily, petting Ruffles, who lay on my chest with her babies.

For some reason, the night before war was always the most peaceful for me.

No nerves.

No worries.

No doubts.

Tomorrow, I would leave to the underworld with my pack warriors and fight for everything that Aurora and I had built here on earth. No matter what happened down there, I would survive and come back to our baby, who I probably wouldn't see before I left.

Aurora might be heavily pregnant, but we would be leaving for the underworld in less than five hours, which meant that our baby would either come very soon or Aurora would stay here until she gave birth and then meet us in the underworld below.

It was risky, and I didn't want to leave her, for fear that I wouldn't see her again, but it had to be done. Time was up. War was here. We either fought hard or we died, and I refused to lose this war.

I never lost a war.

Maybe battles, but never war.

Intertwining my fingers with hers, I smiled and closed my eyes. And somewhere along the way, I would find Mars, so we could be a happy family once more. I was ready for tomorrow. More ready than I had ever been.

We would win.

CHAPTER 37

AURORA

For the first night in over a month, Ares slept soundly beside me without tossing and turning in bed, those foul nightmares hopefully gone—or at least easing. I curled up into the crook of his arm as Frito, Funyun, Cheeto, and Dorito lay down in a line on his bare chest. Ruffles lay on me, twisting up around my swollen belly with one paw on my stomach.

Our alarm rang through the darkness, and I whimpered at my lack of sleep. While Ares might've had a quiet night, mine had been plagued with doubts and worries. I slammed my hand down on the side table and reached for my phone.

It tumbled to the ground with a thud, the alarm still ringing out into the darkness. Ruffles opened one eye, annoyed, and jumped off the bed to swat the alarm off with her paw. I turned onto my side and kissed Ares's neck.

"Ares," I whispered, fingers coiling around his abdomen, "I'm … I'm not ready for today."

Ares intertwined our fingers and stroked his thumb against

mine, his voice gruff. "Well, you're not going down to the underworld until our baby is born, so you might not even be going today, Kitten."

"But you will be," I whispered, tears welling up in my eyes. "I'm so scared."

When Ares turned onto his side, all the kittens slid down his abs and onto the mattress between us. Ruffles tugged them onto me and lay them around my belly, and then she took a seat on my hips, just below my bump.

A streak of light flooded into the room from the break between the curtains, sitting diagonally across Ares's face. His brown eyes transformed in the sudden light, becoming a mess of golds, browns, and hazel.

"Don't be scared, Kitten," Ares said, brushing some hair from my face. "We might have to leave everyone behind, but we will be back, no matter what. We're going down into the underworld to save the wolf species and end this war once and for all. And maybe, along the way, we'll find Mars too."

"Mars," I whispered. "We have to come back. Mars needs to meet our baby."

After lying in bed for a few more moments, Ares turned his back to me, leaned over the side of the bed, and pulled open the drawer under the bed. "I almost forgot that I have something to give the kittens before we leave."

Once he turned back to me, he laid out four small, colorful hats.

Green. Yellow. Red. Purple.

Giggles escaped my lips, bubbling from my belly. "Where did you get all these hats?"

Ares smirked and glanced down at me. "That's my little secret."

Ruffles brushed against him and purred as a thank-you, and then she grabbed the hats in her mouth and matched the hats to each of her babies. Frito, green. Funyun, yellow. Cheeto, red. Dorito, purple.

I grinned and shook my head at Ares. I didn't know how he did it all the time, but he could make me happy when I felt the absolute worst. He might've thought that he couldn't become the man I needed after Mars left, but damn, he had become more than that.

He had become everything to me.

"You're a dork," I said to him, helping Ruffles fasten the hats on her kittens.

"I'd be anything for you," Ares said. He grabbed my hand and pulled me to my feet, and then he wrapped an arm around my waist and pressed his lips on mine. His lips tasted like hazelnut, moving softly against mine, his sweet scent coasting around my body and entangling me.

This wasn't like a kiss Ares had ever given me.

This was filled with fiery passion and undeniable love.

He swept his hands up my body and gently cupped my face, the soft strokes of his thumbs sending shivers through me. I breathed into the kiss, wanting and aching for more of him because I didn't know when I'd give birth and follow him to the underworld.

When I finally pulled away for a breath, my lips lingered on his.

"All I want you to be for me is yourself," I whispered, warmth exploding throughout my chest. "You're everything that I could ever hope for in a man, in a mate, and in a father, Ares. Don't let anyone, even that mind of yours, tell you otherwise."

"Kitten," he whispered, his gruff voice turning soft, "I'm going to miss this." He wrapped his fingers around the back of my neck and stared around the room. "These quiet and early mornings, curled up in our bed, where I get to hold you without a worry in the world, seeing you carry my pup."

I'd promised myself that I wouldn't cry today, so I pushed my tears away. Instead, I grabbed his hand and intertwined our fingers together, holding them close to my chest. "We'll come back to this, Ares." I kissed our hands. "I'm only and forever yours."

"Forever yours," he repeated. "Forever yours, Kitten."

"*Meow*," Ruffles added, as if she wanted to be forever ours too.

Again, I giggled and glanced back at her lying in the center of her kittens. She closed her eyes in utter bliss and purred loudly, setting off her other kittens to purr, too, the sound conquering that of the other packs gathering outside.

"We should go," I said, glancing toward the window. "It sounds like the alphas are already outside to leave for the underworld soon. We have to say our good-byes to everyone."

Once we dressed and picked up the kittens, we walked with Ruffles outside the pack house. Hundreds of people stood around, hugging and kissing each other good-bye, tears pouring down their cheeks.

I teetered on my feet, my stomach twisting with nerves, and placed down the kittens.

Today was really the day.

"Aurora!" Elijah shouted, jogging up toward me with Adrian and then pulling me into a tight hug. "Be careful down there." He rocked us back and forth, not letting go. "I promised Jeremy that I'd protect you, but ... you're stronger than all of us. You'll be the one protecting us. I just need you to come back."

"I promise that when I come back, we can go to the cave and remember everything that Jeremy was. He won't be forgotten by me, no matter how long we're down there." I pulled away and stared up into his glossy brown eyes. Ruffles brushed against me. "And please take care of Ruffles while we're gone."

"Of course."

Ruffles glared at me, picked her babies up by the back of their necks, and forced them all to stand next to her. Stand tall.

Usually, kittens couldn't even open their eyes until eight days after they were born, and Ruffles had made them all stand.

It shouldn't be possible.

I arched my brow. "Are you going to be good for Elijah?"

"*Meow.*"

"Ruffles, you can't come with us."

"*Meow.*"

"Ruffles, you have babies to take care of."

"*Meow.*"

"They can't come with you."

After meowing one last time, Ruffles turned away and licked her children. I massaged the creases on my forehead from the stress of today and glanced over at Ares, who crouched down and petted Funyun.

He looked up at me. "What?"

"We can't let her bring her litter down to the underworld."

"Ruffles is just as stubborn as you. She's going to do what she wants."

"Ruffles," I started, "please, just stay here."

"*Meow,*" she said in that sassy attitude of hers, turning her butt toward me to show me that she was done with this conversation. Her tail swayed side to side as Pringle hurried over to her and dropped a bunch of cat treats at her feet, as if she were some kind of goddess to him.

What a little ho.

"No!" Charolette shouted to my left.

Ares and I glanced over our shoulders in her direction. Streaks of black mascara stained her flushed cheeks, accompanied by dark circles under her eyes. She shook her head from side to side and hit Marcel in the chest.

"You can't go!" she shouted, tears pouring down her cheeks. "You can't!"

My chest tightened at the thought of this being Marcel's last moment with Charolette. Charolette was crying and begging him to stay with her until the day she died. Her fragile and bruised body clinging on to him, her sickness taking her by storm.

"Please, Marcel, at least mark me."

Marcel rubbed her shoulders and bit back tears. "I can't," he whispered.

"I'm begging you," she pleaded.

"I can't, Charolette."

Again, she balled her hand into a small fist and punched his chest, her knuckles bruising. "Why are you leaving?" Charolette asked through her sobs. She shook her head, as if she didn't believe he was really leaving, and stepped away from him, pointing a finger at him. "You can't go, Marcel. You can't leave me here alone! It's not fair."

"Charolette," Marcel whispered, tucking some hair behind her ear.

She hit his hand away. "No! Don't *Charolette* me! You're my mate, and you're leaving me. I only have a few more weeks left to live, and you … you don't want to spend them with me?!" She took another step away from him, further rejecting his attempts to calm her down. "Why?" she whispered, voice cracking. "Why won't you stay a bit longer?"

A strained expression crossed his wavering face. "I can't stay with you."

She smacked him across the face. "You're selfish. You don't want to see me dwindle away. You don't want to be here to support your mate during the hardest of fucking times. I should've never fallen in love with you. I should've left you before this started!"

Before he could pull her toward him, she stormed toward the pack house. "You are a terrible mate. You don't deserve any of the time we've spent together. I hate you, Marcel. I will always hate you for this!"

When she slammed the pack house door, I hurried over to Marcel. With pain etched on every inch of his sculpted face, he slumped his shoulders forward and clutched his chest, lips trembling.

"Marcel, she doesn't mean that. If she knew what you were doing for her, she'd know how selfless you are. Don't let her—"

Marcel tore himself away from me, shifted into his silver wolf, and sprinted through the woods, howling out harrowingly to the dawn sky. I wanted to run after him, but he disappeared into the sea of trees.

From the outskirts of the crowded clearing, I stared into the forest with tears in my eyes. Suddenly, a pain split through my stomach, so intensely that I doubled over onto my knees.

Ares quickly wrapped his arms around me to hold me up and furrowed his brows. "Aurora, what's—"

I grasped his bicep tightly, my claws ripping through his light fall jacket. "Holy fuck."

"Aurora," Medusa called, hurrying through the crowd. When she reached me, she pulled the veil back and stared me in the eyes, pushing some hair from my now-sweating face. "Aurora, what's wrong?"

"The baby," I whispered, gathering enough strength to stand, turn, and fall into Ares's arms again. Why hadn't I felt this before? Where were the contractions? Why had it started so suddenly? Another pain split through my stomach. "The baby, I think she's coming."

Ares scooped me up into his arms and headed toward the hospital, but I grabbed on to him and shook my head. "Just take me inside the pack house. We—we don't have time. The baby is about to—"

I howled to the sky, my pelvis feeling like it was being ripped open.

"Take her inside," Medusa instructed Ares.

Despite wanting to bring me to the hospital, Ares rushed into the house with me and laid me on our bed. Ruffles and her kittens hurried into the room with us, gathering by the door and stopping Elijah and the others from entering.

Medusa pushed up the bottom of my flowy dress. "Sweetie, you have to push right now."

Tears flowed down my cheeks from the agonizing pressure. I gripped onto the thin bedsheets and threw my head back, the intense feeling worse than I'd expected. Was birthing a goddess harder than birthing a human?

None of the books I'd read said it'd hurt *this* badly.

I thought that with my powers, I'd be able to birth with ease, not like this.

Ares knelt by the bedside and pushed some hair off my sweaty forehead. "Shh, shh, shh, Kitten. You can do this," he mumbled into my ear, holding one of my hands tightly and placing his other on my stomach to rub soothing circles around it. "Come on. Push for us and for our baby."

Medusa stood between my legs, holding out her hands and staring at me with tears in her eyes. "Aurora, I never really told you this, but I know how hard it is to do what you're about to do. When I gave you up, I had so much pain inside my heart for years."

I screamed out to the gods and pushed hard, my vagina throbbing and cramping.

"When your mother sent me pictures of you, I would cry for days," Medusa continued, spreading my legs slightly. "I missed every single one of your holidays, birthdays ... every day. I wanted to see you so badly. I thought about you every morning, afternoon, and night."

After clutching onto Ares's hand and squeezing, I pushed hard and screamed out loud again. Ruffles jumped onto the bed and brushed herself against me, her gray fur rubbing against my bare belly. Medusa spread my legs even wider and shouted for someone to get a nurse or doctor.

"Not being able to see you or touch you ruined me," Medusa said. "Push."

"Harder," Ares said, glancing between my legs with glossy eyes. "One more push."

Gasping for air, I stared down at Medusa with tears in my eyes and pushed. "Why are you telling me this now?"

Medusa pressed her thin lips together. "Because you were right. I do regret leaving you."

My vagina split open, tears poured down my cheeks, and a baby cried. I crushed Ares's hand and gave one final push, letting my baby come to life. My chest heaved up and down uncontrollably, the pressure still intense between my legs.

"Kitten," Ares whispered to me, still rubbing my stomach but now staring at our baby in Medusa's arms. A tear rolled down the god of war's cheek, and a breathtaking smile graced my mate's face. "She's beautiful."

I lifted my arms for her, eager to hold my daughter. "Let me see her."

All I wanted was to hold her one time before I had to give her away.

"I know that you will never forgive me for this," Medusa said, cradling my baby in her arms. She glanced down at her with tears in her eyes and then looked back up at me. "But this is what needs to be done."

When I reached out to touch my baby's small, delicate hand before I had to leave her forever, Medusa snatched her away from me. A mist fabricated around Medusa, her body thinning, almost as if she had never even been here.

"I'm sorry," she whispered right before she vanished into thin air.

Stumbling out of the bed, I shook my head and desperately grasped the air where she had once inhabited. It was empty, completely and utterly empty. She'd just disappeared with my child in her arms.

"No!" I screamed. "No! No! No! No! No! No!"

Wailing at the top of my lungs, I tried frantically to scramble to my feet, but birthing a god had made me weak. And Medusa had known that when she stole my baby before I even had a chance to hold her. She'd fucking known it.

I collapsed over the red-stained bed, my stomach tight and blood gushing between my legs.

"Medusa!" I screamed, the sound echoing throughout the entire pack house. Tears streamed down my face. "Medusa! Give me my baby back."

A nurse hurried into the room with wide eyes and worry etched on her face. "She needs to calm down now. Help her calm down, Alpha. If she keeps this up, she might start hyperventilating."

"Give me my daughter back!" I screamed out to nothingness, voice trembling.

Ares wrapped his arms around me and pulled my head to his chest. "Kitten, calm down," he said, though he was choked up too. "Your heart rate is rising quickly. You have to calm down and breathe."

I grabbed onto him like he was the only thing I had left and let out a howl. "All I wanted to do was hold her." My body trembled back and forth. "I just wanted to hold my baby girl and promise her that I'd be back. I didn't get to do either! Medusa will pay for this. She will fucking pay!"

CHAPTER 38

AURORA

*G*rasping onto Ares's hand, I pulled myself to a standing position and kept myself steady. Blood rolled down my thighs and pooled under me. I pushed a hand between my legs and used my power to heal myself the best that I could with the little strength I had left.

I wanted Ares to go get our daughter—just to hold her one time, for both our sakes—but I wanted to go with him, too, and I knew that he wouldn't leave my side even if I begged him to go see her. He should, but he wouldn't.

Ares wrapped his arm around my waist and gently stroked his thumb against the dress plastered on my hip from the blood. "Kitten," he whispered to me, his nose against my ear. Every bit of him was tense, even his voice.

Ruffles rushed into the room, looking from me to the door. "*Meow.*" All her babies, except Frito, were standing next to her and rubbing against me. She moved Dorito away from me and nudged the back of my leg. "*Meow.*"

She wanted me to see something, but I couldn't think straight.

All I could focus on was finding Medusa and killing her for this.

Suddenly, a thunderous boom echoed throughout the room, making the house quake. The only time I had heard that sound before was when we were trapped in those underground tunnels, waiting impatiently for those from the underworld to leave.

Medusa must've turned everyone to stone here. Now.

That must mean that she was within a few miles.

We had to find her.

Ares helped me hobble to the front door as quickly as I could. I didn't know what to say to him. We were both mourning the loss of our baby and the betrayal of the woman who was supposed to be my mother.

All I had wanted to do was see our baby, give her a name, and grasp her tiny fingers.

That was all.

For fuck's sake, I was giving up my own daughter. Medusa had convinced me to do it. The least she could have done was let me see her face. I deserved that much, right? Who was I going to know who to fight for? Who was I going to know who to come back to?

After I ripped the front door open, my knees buckled from the sheer amount of blood I had lost from a baby ripping its way out of my vagina to the shock of seeing everyone—even the alphas who were here to say good-bye and supposed to stay behind—as stone in our front yard.

From the alphas who were supposed to stay to Elijah and Adrian, even Frito.

Stone.

All fucking stone.

Ruffles ran over to Frito and licked his tiny face, her body and the small bodies of her kittens curling around Frito, as if it would bring him back to life. But there weren't many people who came back to life after traveling to the underworld. I didn't even know if it was possible for anyone without the help of Medusa, except divine beings.

Charolette hurried out of the house after us and doubled over Marcel's stone wolf, screaming and crying to the Moon Goddess. "No! Marcel! I'm sorry for telling you that I hated you. I'm sorry for being a bitch to you. I just …" She brushed her fingers against his stone snout. "Please, come back to me. Please."

"Stand up, Charolette," Ares snarled, grabbing her by the waist, pulling her to her feet, and steadying her. "You need to lead this pack now. Make sure you all survive while we're trying to save the fucking world."

Charolette widened her eyes. "B-but I'm going to die in—"

Ares growled again, the sound echoing through the now eerily silent forest. "Lead!"

That was his last word to her. After grabbing my hand, he pulled me toward the forest to Vulcan's pack house, where Medusa had to have gone to give the baby to them. Ruffles meowed, and then twenty little footsteps—including Funyun's, Cheeto's, Dorito's, Frito's and Pringles's—followed behind us, jogging to keep up.

Tears blurred my vision. Tree branches scraped my arms. I continued to run, no matter what, picking up my pace, the closer we approached Vulcan's property. While I couldn't shift at the moment, I knew Ares ached to transform into his wolf and tear up the world to find his daughter.

"Right over here," Ares said, nodding ahead. "Come on."

To my surprise, we reached the edge of Vulcan's property before anyone caught sight of us. And just as we crossed over into his property and approached the pack house, I saw Venus holding our daughter closer to her chest and grinning up at Vulcan.

As I howled to the gray sky, Medusa opened the pack house's front door, unveiled her face, and looked me and Ares dead in the eye. I lunged toward her, desperate to rip her to shreds for what she had done. She murmured in ancient Latin, and suddenly, my body and Ares's body was stopping mid-stride. My muscles were solidifying, my body turning to stone.

"Medusa," I said through a mouth that I couldn't seem to move anymore, "I will kill you for this. I will kill you!"

CHAPTER 39

ARES

*E*verything went dark.

One moment passed, then two, and then I landed with a thud on broken, dry ground. Hundreds of warriors that had been cemented in stone at our pack house stood around us, all speaking in hushed tones and careful not to alert the monstrous creatures lurking in this foggy land.

The beasts looked like wild, savage monsters who had traveled these lands for far too long. Too fat, too tall, too broken, too zombie-like to live on the ground above, on earth, a place I wasn't sure we'd ever return to.

After Ruffles reunited her babies with Frito, Aurora appeared beside me a moment later, her arm immediately looping around mine. She inched closer to me and bit her lip, trying hard to stop her sobs from breaking through the quietness.

"It's coming," a sea of whispers echoed through the lands. "The ferry is coming."

I grasped her hand tighter and pushed my way through the

warriors until we reached the front. From the corner of my eye, I saw Marcel lurking behind the blackened, charcoaled trees. He nodded to me, and I nodded back to thank him for all he was doing for me, for my sister, and for our family.

He was making the ultimate sacrifice.

When I turned back, a half-human, half-skeleton–looking man who must be Charon stood on the small wooden boat with an oar in his hand and a black hood covering his head. If the oar in his hand were a scythe, he'd almost look like the Grim Reaper from this distance.

Everyone behind me turned silent when he docked the boat on the edge of the river and looked in our direction.

"A coin for your travels," he said, voice coming out hoarse and raspy. When he spoke, he tilted his head up to the side just slightly, and I saw the jagged tooth in his skeleton mouth.

With a canine that large, was he part wolf?

"One coin per traveler," he continued.

I stuffed my hands into my pocket, finding a spare coin that I knew I hadn't had before. Someone must've put it there. Aurora pulled one out of her pocket, too, and stared down at it with wide eyes. It wasn't a normal human coin, but one that I didn't recognize despite my travels far and wide to find the stone.

After swallowing my fear, I placed the coin in his hand and looked him dead in the eye. Though I expected to see someone cold staring back at me, I saw the eyes of Charolette and froze. When he looked away, I shook my head. It hadn't even been twenty minutes yet, and I already missed her so fucking much that I was seeing her in other people. Was that what the underworld did to wolves like me?

He held out his bony hand for Aurora to place her coin in. She stared at it and swallowed hard.

"Ares, I-I don't know if I can do this …" she said, but I knew she wasn't talking about being in the underworld. She was talking about being without our daughter.

I didn't want her to know that this was hurting me too. She had been there for me so many times when I didn't feel good enough. She had supported me during my darkest times when I felt like the world was crashing down upon me. I wanted to be that rock for her too.

Maybe I should've broken down and cried, but I hadn't just given birth and had our baby stolen without seeing her first. I'd caught a glimpse of her face—those small pink lips and unruly black hair and eyes so bright, just like Aurora's.

After grabbing Aurora's hand, I placed the coin in Charon's hand for her, walked with her to the boat, and led the way for the warriors behind me. "The only way back is to fight," I said to her.

We didn't know the first thing about being gods, our true potential, or the powers we possessed. But we would learn, and we'd be back for the girl who we loved more than anything.

To be continued in *Only Yours, Alpha* ...
Pre Order *Only Yours, Alpha* now: https://books2read.
com/u/38dk6B
OR
Start reading *Only Yours, Alpha* now: https://www.
patreon.com/emiliarosewriting

ALSO BY EMILIA ROSE

Submitting to the Alpha

Defying the Alpha

Alpha Maddox

Nyx

On Patreon

Poison

Mafia Boss

My Werewolf Professor

The Twins

Excite Me Trilogy

ABOUT THE AUTHOR

Emilia Rose is an international best-selling author of steamy paranormal romance. Highly inspired by her study abroad trip to Greece in 2019, Emilia loves to include Greek and Roman mythology in her writing.

She graduated from the University of Pittsburgh with a degree in psychology and a minor in creative writing in 2020 and now writes novels as her day job.

With over eighteen million combined story views online and a growing presence on reading apps, she hopes to inspire other young novelists with her journey of growth and imagination so that they go on to write the books that need to be told.

STAY CONNECTED

Subscribe to Emilia's newsletter for exclusive news >
https://www.emiliarosewriting.com/

Chat with fans, participate in giveaways, and get more here >
https://discord.gg/TsSK3V8Tdh